Tara's Secret

Tara's Secret

A Novel

WILLIAM GARLINGTON

WHITE CLOUD PRESS
ASHLAND, OREGON

Printed in Canada

First White Cloud Press edition: 2003

Cover art: Kilimba Goravani

ISBN: 1-883991-50-1

Library of Congress Cataloging-in-Publication Data

Garlington, William, 1947-
    Tara's secret: a novel / William Garlington
      p. cm.
    ISBN 1-883991-50-1
      1. Teacher-student relationships–Fiction 2. Spiritual life–Fiction.
    3. Priests–Fiction. 4. India–Fiction. I. Title

    PS3557.A7164T37 2003
    813'.54--dc21

                                              2003043076

Although several of the characters in this story have been influenced
in part by the lives and ideas (as expressed in certain religious texts
and speeches) of specific historical figures, they remain primarily the
fictional creations of the author.

Chapter 1

Ishakpur was an old village. Tradition recorded that the hamlet had been founded by a group of wandering pujari brahmans some five hundred years before the arrival of the British in India. While it was certainly true that tradition was not always the most accurate source of information, it was essentially the only fund of knowledge the villagers could call upon for formulating the how's and why's of their community's roots. One thing was certain: several of the most prominent brahman families could trace their village ancestry back at least nine generations, and when it came to establishing the antiquity of a place, the region's genealogists were virtually unanimous in considering seven generations to be a legitimate index.

Ishakpur was comprised of a conglomeration of small dwellings, primarily composed of wooden supports, mud and straw plaster walls, and thatched roofs linked together by a winding and seemingly endless series of very narrow dirt lanes which, depending on the season, were filled with either mud or chalk-fine dust. Surrounding the clusters of houses, like an assortment of oversized, fully-opened umbrellas, were large numbers of massive old banyan trees whose blanketing shade was the only protection the village's inhabitants could hope for from the penetrating heat of the noonday sun.

Beyond the trees and stretching in all four directions, acre upon acre of Ishakpur's wheat and sorghum fields sprawled forth in a series of uneven parcels that resembled an awkwardly patched quilt. About one quarter of a mile away from the village's southern-most dwellings, the languid water of a small shallow stream slowly meandered its way westward. The rivulet was a source of irrigation for the constantly thirsty fields as well as a washing spot for both humans and animals. For most of the year it was little more than a large pond. Only during the months of the monsoon, when water seemingly poured from the sky in buckets, was its channel completely bursting.

The village's main well was located near the center of the hamlet just across the square from an unpretentious temple that housed the hand-carved wooden images of Krishna and his divine consort, Radha. Here the women of the upper castes, mainly brahmans and rajputs, gathered in small groups throughout the course of the day to obtain water for their households and share with each other the latest gossip. Since major events in Ishakpur were generally lacking, the stories were often embellished by the speakers' imaginative interpretations.

It was at this well on a hot but cloudy day late in the summer of the year 1861 that three young women from the rajput caste were busily drawing water and chatting with one another about Ishakpur's latest gossip. All of them were attired in multi-colored saris that gracefully wrapped their bodies from neck to feet, revealing only the flesh of their heavily bangled arms and ankles and brief glimpses of their light-brown bellies. The reds, yellows, purples, oranges, and blues of the garments contrasted sharply with the drab earthiness of their surroundings.

"I suppose you have heard about that naughty rascal, Bakshi Ram?" the heftiest of the women interjected while placing her brass pot on the ground and adjusting the top of her blue and green sari.

"No bhai," responded the woman in a red and yellow garment who was drawing water. "Do tell us."

The youngest and most attractive of the three women let out a brief, high-pitched giggle and then replied. "You always seem to know everything that is happening with the pujari men, Rituji!"

"Well Rani bhai, I just keep my ears open. I can't help what comes in." Ritu smiled broadly, as did the others.

"Come on, tell us," the woman at the well demanded. "You know it's not proper to keep secrets from your kinfolk." Again the three shared a common smile.

"Well," Ritu began, "from what I understand, Bakshi Ram has lately been seen by several reliable sources humping a young chamar woman down by the river late at night. Apparently, she gives him a special sign by banging on her water pot when the coast is clear."

"Well, if what you say is true Ritu bhai, it would seem that it is more than her water pot that is getting banged." Rani chuckled. "But I must ask. Who are these sources that tell you such things?"

"My lips are sealed to secrecy."

"Such promises have never stopped you before." Rani looked coyly at Ritu who pretended she did not hear.

"I have always thought it an advantage not to be allowed to use this well," sighed the woman drawing water, "and this just confirms my judgment. I just can't imagine ever getting the opportunity to be poked around here, can you?" Before she had finished her question, Rani let loose the wooden bucket and allowed it to drop heavily back down into the darkness.

"Shruti, you are indeed a little demon," exclaimed Rani, now unable to contain her laughter. "What in the world would your husband ever say if he were to hear you talking in such a manner?"

"I'm not exactly sure what he might say, my sweet friend, but hopefully it would induce him to poke me a little more often. For as much as he comes to me these days, one would think he is about ready to run off and join those sadhus who are always hanging around the edges of the village with their empty begging bowels. To be honest, I can't even remember the last time my husband became stiff."

"Well, you know what I have heard about those sadhus," Rani boldly interjected. "They are said to have developed marvelous powers of self-control. A woman from a village not far from here told me about one such holy man who was able to keep his own staff standing as erect as that Shiva lingam over there for more than two hours." She simultaneously pointed at the semi-elliptical orange and silver stone that sat in the shade of nearby banyan tree.

"And you have the nerve to tell me I am a gossip?" exclaimed Ritu. "Those holy men have been known to cast harmful spells on people, you know, so I wouldn't talk too loudly if I were you."

"Well, Bakshi Ram might not be able to cast an evil spell on you," answered Rani abruptly, "but I am certain he would not be very pleased to know that you are spreading news around the village of his illicit conquests, especially with an untouchable woman. You know that he could be in a great deal of trouble if the pujari caste elders were to find out about it."

Ritu glanced quickly downward and scraped purposefully at the dust with her over-sized and leathery big toe. "Well, for your information, I was told that he already has an answer prepared."

Neither Shruti nor Rani bothered to offer a response, but their silence asked their question for them.

"Can you believe it," Ritu continued, now scanning the square as she spoke, "that scoundrel Bakshi Ram had the nerve to tell one of my girlfriends that although he may have humped the chamar woman several times, he has never once allowed himself to take food or water from her hands."

All three women laughed heartily. "Only from the mouth of a pujari could one hear such an explanation," exclaimed Shruti. "I swear that a pujari could argue that day is night and night is day."

"And what is more," Rani added, "he could undoubtedly find a religious text to support him."

"You will get no argument here," Ritu agreed.

By this time, Shruti had taken her dripping clay pot and placed it at her feet. Rani knew that she could now take her turn at the well. In the manner of her two companions, Rani set her own pot on the well's edge, took hold of the worn rope that was attached to the rickety wooden bucket, and, hand over hand, gradually lowered it until she heard a soft splashing sound from the depths below. The container slowly filled with the precious liquid. Rani looked up from her task to see a young boy emerging into Ishakpur's main square from the shadows of one of the nearby lanes. He was barefoot and shirtless and stood a little over five feet in height. His white cotton dhoti draped his upper legs. Its greyish shade indicated that it had likely not been cleaned for some time. As the lad came ever closer, the women could behold both the three-stranded sacred thread, which encircled his torso by falling diagonally from left shoulder to right hip and then up across the sinewy muscles in his back, and his loosely hanging necklace of large black tulsi beads.

"So, here comes little Gopala," Rani suddenly announced. "Now if you want to talk about a strange pujari . . ."

Everyone in Ishakpur knew Gopala's story: One night, fifteen years earlier, when his aging father was away on an extended business trip to Benares, his barren mother had made a clandestine pilgrimage to a local shrine dedicated to the elephant-headed god, Ganesh. There, she claimed, the god had told to her she would soon bear a very special child who if guided properly would reveal to the world a great secret. The tale took on some degree of credence when a year later Gopala was born on the day of the Ganesh Chaturi Festival.

As soon as he could speak, the little boy displayed a precociousness that led many of Ishakpur's villagers to treat him with an awe-filled, yet distanced, respect. But when he was ten, Gopala's father suddenly died under rather mysterious circumstances in a nearby town; some whispered in the arms of a temple prostitute.

Not long after his father's ashes had been spread, the boy began falling into trance-like states that would last for several hours. By the time he received his sacred thread, the symbol of his initiation into manhood, Gopala had abandoned his traditional religious studies and started spending more and more time with the sadhus. He would secretly meet up with them on the outskirts of the village and thereafter wander freely throughout the various wards of the community, sometimes singing, sometimes dancing, and sometimes just staring off into space as if oblivious to his surroundings.

To many, these were all signs that Gopala was indeed a sacred child, but to others they were indications that something was very wrong with both the boy and his family. It was not a case of divine conception, these skeptics believed, but of possibilities much more dark and insidious. Only a mixture of caste blood, or perhaps something even worse, could produce such dire results.

"What the boy needs is a wife," said Shruti, "someone who can take that energy and put it where it belongs."

Rani's reply was prompt. "For as horny as you sound these days, you could probably do the job Shrutiji."

Shruti gave Rani a playful grimace.

"Well I doubt that such a solution would work in any case," Ritu blithely responded. "From everything I have heard, young Gopala seems to like boys much better than he does girls."

Rani nodded her head in agreement. "If he were a woman, he would no doubt want to marry his friend, Ram Das. You must have seen them playing together like they were Radha and Krishna."

The young intruder was now close enough to the three women that they could clearly make out the characteristics of his appearance which, except for his eyes, were by-in-large inconspicuous from those of most of the other boys in the village: unobtrusive chin, balanced cheek bones, nondescript nose, close-cropped jet-black hair. But the eyes could not be missed. The greyish-blue orbs, unusual even for pujaris, sat awkwardly high on his mocha-colored face and seemed overly large for the rest of his head. At the moment, they were darting wildly from side to side as if they were following the movements of a flitting bird or insect.

"He has been with the sadhus again," murmured Shruti. "Look at those smudgy ash marks on his forehead."

"You are right," confirmed Rani.

"Hey Gopala." Ritu shouted.

The woman's voice appeared to momentarily stun Gopala. He stopped in his tracks and looked vaguely over in the direction of the well. He stood still and squinted, seemingly to allow his eyes time to adjust to the new setting. "Hail O gopis," he replied in a loud and shrill voice. "Hail, O magnificent Chandravali, hail O beautiful Lalita, hail O wondrous Champakalata." Then just as suddenly as he had stopped, Gopala directed his eyes skyward, shuffled his feet together, and continued undisturbed across the square.

The women giggled. "See what I mean," said Rani. "He thinks we are gopis."

"Well, I can tell you one thing. I have been called much worse than one of Krishna's divine lovers," Shruti promptly retorted. "And of course it was I whom he referred to as Lalita." She let out a hearty laugh, which the other women recognized as a ploy on her part to hide the fact that she was serious.

The women put the buckets on their heads and prepared to return to their homes. Gopala meanwhile proceeded forward. After he had passed in front of the temple, he veered sharply to his right and entered the mouth of another narrow lane. For a short distance the dusty pathway was relatively straight. It was lined on both sides with tightly-packed houses on whose porches sat small groups of chatting women, their leathery hands rapidly sifting through mounds of newly harvested kernels of wheat. Around and between them, young, half-dressed children romped freely and added their laughs and cries to the constant buzz of their mothers, grandmothers, and aunts' conversations.

Gopala noticed none of these sights and sounds. They may have possibly registered on the periphery of his consciousness, but the focal point of his self-awareness had virtually left him and become lost somewhere deep inside. Only sheer animal reflex, and perhaps the force of habit, could possibly explain how the boy was able to safely maneuver himself forward.

The densely compacted dwellings gave way to more humble abodes and punctuated areas of open space. Around the perimeters of small and well-manicured vegetable gardens, men whose heads were adorned with yellow, white and orange turbans sat together on their haunches, peacefully sharing a smoke from small earthenware pipes. Now and again, an ox-cart filled with either chopped wood or dry patties of cow dung would enter the scene. In pocketed groves, faces of local gods and goddesses stared out from above their flower-strewn altars at the various comings and goings.

Gopala had reached Ishakpur's northernmost boundary. Only a small, slab-stone temple, built in honor of one of the region's local mother goddess, Kshetrapala, and a row of large, gangling banyan trees separated him from the nearly feature-less stretch of wheat and sorghum fields. He was starting to become centered again. The numerous shapes and forms of the surrounding environment were slowly beginning to sharpen in his mind's eye, and he could now feel the muggy and oppressive heat of the late afternoon pressing down upon him.

He sat down on the craggy steps of Kshetrapala's temple and allowed the scene to come into complete focus. Slight traces of anxiety still colored his psyche. Above him two huge crows perched themselves ominously in the banyan trees, call-ing loudly to one another.

Gopala was by now quite used to such inner transitions. His first experience of this phenomenon had occurred shortly after his father's death and had frightened him terribly. But as the years went by, and the frequency of the episodes gradually increased, he had come to accept the fact that he lived in two different worlds whose boundaries were sewn together by ever-so-thin threads of consciousness.

First, there was the phenomenal world of maya—the world of family and village, material success and failure, status and shame, custom and law, wells, temples, shrines, trees, and animals—the world in which he now sat. Then there was the world of lila, the world of divine play, of gods and goddesses, gopis and demons. This was the world where he and Ram Das became Radha and Krishna - the world that adults praised in their most beloved stories but laughed at when displayed be-fore them in the flesh.

More recently, he had become aware of yet another world:

the world of formlessness, the world in which all things seemed to mysteriously merge into one, the world in which his sense of uniqueness was pushed into the background and allowed to drift as if blanketed by a heavy fog, the world from which he had just returned.

Gopala was not consciously aware of what triggered his movements between the first two worlds, but he was fairly sure who led him into this new world: the sadhus. Nearly every time he met with these naked men of spiritual power, whose hardened, sun-scorched bodies had become their own cremation grounds, he was subsequently transported to this third dimension. And whereas he felt entirely comfortable in the world of lila, indeed preferred it to the pretentiousness and callousness of what most ordinary people called the real world, his recent ventures into the formless and timeless void were marked, both before and after, by a heightened degree of apprehension. While there was something quite comforting in the feeling of being totally absorbed, of no longer being the center of the other's gaze, the prospects of the possibility of total annihilation, of never coming back, were frightening. Anxiety attacks had on several occasions led him to promise himself that he would stay completely away from the ascetics, but despite such well-meaning declarations, he had always returned to their company. Their lure had become almost irresistible.

"I must not see them again," Gopala muttered to himself when he was finally in proper command of his thoughts.

But you have said this before, his own mind responded. *You know that you are not strong enough to keep such a promise.*

A growing sense of impotence began to pervade all of Gopala's thoughts. He instinctively understood that the small voice whispering inside his head was correct. In this matter, his will was not under his own control. How many times had he told himself he would never approach the sadhus again? He sat groping for another answer . . . *Then I will make a sacred vow*, he eventually countered, *and I will ask the goddess Kshetrapala for her help.*

Gopala was encouraged by a new surge of revitalized hope

and resolve. He pushed himself up with both of his hands, swiveled his hips in the direction of the temple's entrance, and urgently ascended the unpolished stone stairs. He paused for an instant on the structure's uneven threshold, and then very slowly and deliberately descended into the dark inner sanctum. It took some time for his eyes to become adjusted to the room's lack of light, but gradually Gopala could discern the blurry contours of the stone image as well as the scattered remnants of previous worshipers' offerings. Faded and drying flower petals, random pieces of shriveled coconut meat, and numerous sugar-balls, both large and small, pink and white, littered the water stained altar. He sat down lotus style in front of these oblations and cautiously looked up at the idol. A bulging, white-eyed head sitting atop a six-armed and naked torso stared stoically back at him.

"O Kshetrapala," he whispered, "O mother of plenty. Please give me the strength that I will need to keep this sacred vow; please help me to remain pure in thy sight; please help me to stay away from the sadhus."

Gopala's gaze now centered on the goddess' full, undulating breasts. "O benevolent one, I implore you to grant to your weak child this wish."

Gopala lowered his head and silently waited for a reply. He kept this repose for several minutes. At first, he felt nothing . . . then a sudden shiver of fear swept through his entire body as he remembered that he had forgotten to bring an offering for the goddess. His mind raced . . . the black tulsi beads that the leader of the sadhus had given him were all he had. He removed the necklace and tenderly placed it at the feet of the image. "Please accept this humble offering, O Kshetrapala, as a mark of your servant's most sincere devotion."

The boy peeked a look at Kshetrapala's face. He thought he could detect a smile. He could feel himself becoming calm.

When Gopala exited Kshetrapala's temple the shadows of late afternoon were beginning to slowly blanket the western side of the village, and he knew it was time that he return home. Rather than retrace the route by which he had come, he decided to follow the line of large banyan trees that encircled the hamlet. This course would take him along the edges of the wheat and sorghum fields where he knew he would be less likely to encounter the hustle and bustle of social existence. For although his renewed sense of well-being had lifted his spirits, he still had no desire to engage in human communication.

Half way home Gopala heard a faint fluttering noise in the distance. He looked up to see a flock of snow-white egrets soaring gracefully toward him. He smiled and experienced a tingling sensation wash over his entire body. "O Kshetrapala, O divine goddess, you have set me free," he boldly exclaimed.

In a state of inner excitement Gopala continued to follow the birds' line of flight. Suddenly, from atop the trees located just behind him, two large crows left their perches and flew directly over his head. The black blurs distracted him. He helplessly watched as the squawking crows spiraled upward and then swept down upon the egrets, scattering them in all directions.

Gopala could no longer look. His pace slowed and his head hung earthward. Clarity of thought soon gave way to a growing confusion. His head started to spin. He lurched forward. In an attempt to grab the trunk of a nearby tree, he threw his hands wildly out in front of him, but his right hand slid awkwardly to the side causing him to lose his balance and almost fall to the ground. He stumbled again and then righted himself. "Don't leave," he cried out, "don't leave."

His mind became an uncontrollable kaleidoscope of images that one after another flashed before him: his father's body slowly crumbling apart from the intense heat of the funeral pyre; his mother's Janus face, half sobbing, half smiling; the old sadhu encouraging him to make an offering to the garlanded lingam; Kshetrapala's piercing white eyes seeing through him . . . then all turned pitch black as he collapsed and crumpled helplessly into a heap on the ground.

Two hours later Gopala was found by his friend Ram Das. He was still only partly conscious, and it took some effort for the young boy to get his friend home. They were met by a worried uncle and a virtually hysterical mother who demanded of her son to tell her what he himself did not know: "Why did this happen?"

The woman gave Gopala some tea and put him to bed. "I think he may be crazy," she admitted to her younger brother. "It must be some sort of curse placed upon the family. Perhaps he is paying for his father's sins, . . . or mine. Maybe we have failed to guide him properly."

"Nonsense," the brother replied. "Yes, he is different, but what do you expect of a precocious child? Frankly, I think that you have kept him too much under your wing. Ishakpur is much too small a place for a boy like Gopala. I suggest that you send him to Benares. He can live with our older brother and learn the proper functions of a real pujari. Here, the best he will do is light a few candles and listen to the gossipy women who constantly fill the temple with their jabber."

"I just don't know." The woman sighed and sat down on a short wooden bench. "He seems much too young to be so far away from his mother."

"Then I suggest you pray for an answer. Seek Ganesh's advice."

The woman's spirits immediately picked up. "Yes, you are right," she said. "I should have thought of that myself. Tomorrow I will go to Ganeshji's shrine in Bodhpur. Then I will know what to do."

Chapter 2

Gopala bent to his knees, reached down into the river, and gently scooped up some of its slow-moving water with his cupped hand. While methodically repeating a Vedic mantra, he gradually raised his arm and let the cool liquid spill down onto his head and bare shoulders. Near him hundreds of other men and women of varying ages, sizes, and shapes performed similar rituals, filling the air with a cacophony of sounds as they called out their own sacred verses. And so it had been for hundreds of years on the banks of the Ganges, the heavenly river which legend held as having been brought to earth through the austerities of the ancient sage, Bhagiratha, for the benefit and salvation of the sons and daughters of India.

Gopala completed the last stages of his morning ritual, stood up, straightened his back, and peered out at the bevy of sandstone temples that lined the river's opposite bank. He tarried there briefly, then turned around and hastily strode up the long row of steep steps. On the way he passed countless pilgrims, all of whom were anxious to fill his vacated spot at the water's edge.

Gopala had been in Benares for a little over two years. After a successful visit by his mother to Ganesh's shrine in Bodhpur, and several hours of discussion with various members of the family, including Gopala's older cousin and his maternal grandfather, it was eventually decided that the village was not the best place for the young boy. What he really needed, they had all agreed, was to be in Benares with his uncle. Raychand had been a resident of the city for over five years and could not only teach his nephew the social duties and obligations of a proper pujari brahman, he could also provide him with the emotional and spiritual guidance he so desperately required.

At first Gopala hated his new home, but over time he had come to appreciate the varieties of sense experience that this most holy of cities had to offer. Benares could not simulate the peacefulness of rural fields and groves, yet its sheer size and number of inhabitants allowed for a certain anonymity that a small hamlet like Ishakpur could never provide.

The summit of the bathing steps blended into a wide thoroughfare which, even at this early time of day, was congested not only with people but with a wide variety of animals and conveyances, including scavenging cows, barking dogs, and horse-drawn carriages. For some distance Gopala steadily weaved his way through the oncoming rush of beasts and humanity before changing direction and entering a narrower yet similarly crowded street. On both sides of the avenue, brightly colored billboards covered with broad, black-outlined, devanagri letters announced the wares of the shops below.

Snugly perched above and behind a busy condiment shop was his destination: a two-room office with a small, wooden balcony that overlooked an innocuous side alleyway. Sitting inside the larger of the two rooms at a cluttered desk was Gopala's uncle, Raychand, a tall, handsome man dressed in a long-sleeve cotton shirt and loose-fitting cotton pants.

"Ah, you have finally returned from your morning prayers," his uncle announced when he saw Gopala come through the door. "I must make sure to take care of my own duties soon."

"I would not wait too long if I were you," Gopala replied in a heavy breath. "It won't be very long before it will be almost impossible to reach the water's edge. There are so many pilgrims this time of year, and the large majority of them are virtually heedless of the proper rituals."

Raychand fumbled with a few of the copious papers that lay chaotically strewn across his desk until he located the one he was looking for. He briefly scanned its contents. "I am afraid that we have received some bad news," he said.

Gopala looked at him with raised eyebrows.

"It appears inevitable that I am going to have to close down the business," Raychand said after reading Gopala's face. "The fact of the matter is that there is just not enough revenue to cover the expenses."

Gopala said nothing.

"But do not worry; all is not lost." Raychand grasped another piece of paper and held it up in the air. "I have been in communication with a wealthy gentleman who has recently completed the construction of a school, and he has indicated that he will be in need of several pujaris who have knowledge of the sacred texts. He has agreed to interview me for one of the positions, and if I am fortunate enough to be successful, I am certain that with just a little training you could become my assistant."

"I have other plans."

"And what might those be?" The three lines on Raychand's brown forehead became deep furrows.

"I want to become initiated into the shakta rites at the new Ma Tara temple."

"But that is impossible."

"Why?"

"Because they sacrifice animals there," said Raychand, "and true pujaris should not serve in such temples."

Gopala paced back and forth. "But according to some of the ancient texts, pujaris can serve without blemish in such temples as long as they are not directly involved in the killing of the animal," he said when he had halted. "I have checked this fact with several well-known pujari authorities here in Benares, and they all assure me that there is no specific prohibition to be found in the scriptures. This is why you will find pujaris serving in nearly all temples dedicated to the mahavidya goddesses."

Raychand's face continued to remain expressionless. "If

you ask me, what you are engaging in is nothing more than a mere trick of language," he boldly asserted. "And the fact that you have to rely on the current degraded practices of money-hungry pujaris only compounds the problem."

Gopala could feel his pulse quicken. "For a businessman you certainly seem to have a lot of knowledge about what is religiously proper," he shot back. "Perhaps you should put in more study before you claim to be an authority on such matters."

"Well, I know one thing for certain. Your father would never have agreed to accept such an offer."

"Maybe not, but . . ."

Gopala wanted to say that had it not been for his father's untimely death, they would not have found themselves in this awkward financial situation, but then he thought better of it. "I have already made up my mind," he said instead. "Of course, I would like your support, but I know I am called to serve the goddess."

Raychand did not speak. *He is as willful as ever* he thought.

Gopala broke the silence. "At least come with me tomorrow to the temple grounds and meet the temple owner. There can be no harm in that."

Raychand rose to his feet and dropped the paper on the desk. "I could send you back to Ishakpur," he said.

Gopala stared at him

"But I won't do that. . . . All right, I will meet this man and see for myself. Now it is time for me to go say my morning prayers."

Gopala alighted from the horse-drawn carriage as Raychand hurriedly handed the vehicle's driver two small coins. The young man would have preferred that they walk to their destination, but his uncle was not accustomed to traversing such distances on foot and had ordered the conveyance.

When they were both firmly on the ground, Raychand quietly motioned with his outstretched left hand and then followed Gopala up a gently sloping grass mound which leveled off as it neared the temple's entrance. The two men were soon passing under an arched gateway that was decorated with two huge swastikas. On their right they could see three small temples standing in close proximity to one another. Behind these structures arose the recently finished Ma Tara temple. Its tapering tower of hand-carved stone was capped by fluttering, triangular red and orange flags. On their left lay a rectangular pool of stagnant water in which a scrawny, brown cow was busily quenching its thirst. Straight ahead, at the rear of the compound, sat an impressive, two-story wooden building whose finely chiseled mahogany doors were bordered by a sprawling veranda.

A heavily bearded, white-turbaned servant met them at the foot of the veranda. The man acted as if he were expecting the visitors. He did not bother to question their intent, but ushered them quickly up the brightly polished steps, through the massive doors, and into a spacious waiting room.

"The Master will be with you in a few moments," the servant said. He made a half-hearted bow and rapidly departed through an adjacent doorway.

Before Raychand and Gopala had time to survey the room the same doorway was filled with the figure of another man. He was dressed in a light-blue, silk coat that fell almost to the middle of his thighs and covered the top half of his matching pajama pants. The coat was drawn to his body at the waist by a yellow and brown sash that mirrored in both color and pattern the fanciful turban adorning his head. Although he was more than slightly overweight, his height, which measured over six feet, somewhat countered the excesses of fine dining, giving him an appearance of both strength and formidability. His delicate hands were drawn tightly together at his chest; his strikingly handsome face tilted slightly downwards.

"You must be Raychand," the man exclaimed in a deep and slightly raspy voice. "Your dear nephew often speaks of you with great warmth and respect. It is obvious that he holds you in high esteem . . . Welcome to our temple."

Raychand bent slightly forward and politely returned the

man's salutation. "Thank you for taking the time to meet with me."

"Let me introduce myself," the man continued as he moved forward into the room. "I am Harish, owner of the temple estate. I have had the privilege of meeting your nephew, and he has very much impressed me, not only with his knowledge of the sacred texts but with, . . . how might I say it . . . his innate spirituality."

Harish stared piercingly at Gopala, noticing every feature of his young face. At first, the boy looked back at his purveyor, but when the man's gaze did not retreat, he eventually glanced downward.

"He has always taken his religious duties very seriously." Raychand's words recaptured the older man's attention.

Raychand had promised Gopala that he would not voice his objections immediately, but now he instinctively expressed his concern to the stately gentleman. "I apologize if I speak boldly," he said, "but my nephew has informed me that he desires to be initiated into the shakta priesthood of your temple, and I must be honest in telling you that I have strong reservations about his serving in a temple where animal sacrifice is practiced."

Gopala was horrified and instantly thought about how he might rectify the potential disaster. But Harish was seemingly unbothered by the question. He filled his face with a Cheshire-like smile. "There is nothing to apologize for," he answered. "You are entitled to your opinions, but of one thing I can assure you: there is nothing done at this temple that is not in complete accordance with the sacred texts. Moreover, although this has not been made common knowledge, I will let you in on a little secret. Ma Tara herself requested that this temple be built. Several years ago the holy goddess appeared to this humble servant in a dream and told me that if a temple were constructed at this site in her honor then she would manifest herself in the image." Harish's eyes widened. "She also said that one day her temple would become famous throughout all of India."

When Harish saw no response in Raychand's face, he

paused briefly to gather some new thoughts.

"In any case," he quickly continued, "when it comes to matters of ritual law we must expect some degree of relativity. These things are strictly matters of maya, no doubt necessary on the mundane level, but certainly in no way capable of limiting Tara's divine power. Even the Lord Shiva himself cannot do that!"

Harish seemed pleased with this comment and once again covered his face with a huge grin. "Indeed, your nephew's coming to know about the temple is auspicious. Such things do not happen simply by chance. It is clear to me that the goddess has chosen Gopala to become her servant."

During Harish's brief oration, Gopala had suddenly begun to experience a slight faintness in his head. Now that the man was silent, a distinct dizziness enveloped the boy's being. Not since he left Ishakpur had this feeling come upon Gopala. He tried mightily to ward it off, but to no avail. His skin became moist; the room began to spin. He looked up at Harish. The temple owner's head had become a magnified but blurry mass. The face was nearly gone . . . Gopala gasped for breath . . . the words, *her servant*, kept repeating themselves over and over in his ears. He rocked back and forth. He felt that he might fall.

Raychand noticed what was happening. He reached out and grabbed Gopala by the shoulders. "It must be the heat," he said.

Harish said nothing while privately thinking that Gopala's near swoon was an obvious sign sent to him by the goddess indicating her approval.

"Come, bring the boy over here," the temple owner said at last. He pointed excitedly to a nearby divan. "I will have my servant bring him some water." He clapped his hands loudly several times.

Raychand helped usher the still wobbly Gopala to the divan and sat down beside him, all the while keeping a firm grasp on the boy's arm.

"You called Sahib?" the servant asked as he entered the room.

"Quickly Sumai, bring some cold water for the boy,"

Harish called out in a loud and demanding voice.

The servant bowed and departed.

By the time Sumai had returned with a dripping brass cup Gopala was sitting up straight The spinning sensation had left him, and he was again able to recognize where he was.

Raychand let go of Gopala's arm and prepared to offer an apology to Harish, but his plans were interrupted when the temple owner announced his own thoughts: "Your question has just been answered. My mention of the goddess' call has caused your nephew to swoon. This is certainly a sign of divine confirmation. Gopala can move into the acolyte's quarters tomorrow evening. Sumai will show you where they are located. For the moment, I have some business to attend to in the city, so I must excuse myself."

Raychand was speechless. He watched Harish bring his hands to his mouth and make a slight bow.

Chapter 3

Gopala left his room in the building directly across from the pujaris' living quarters, quietly crossed the large brick courtyard, and reverently approached the side door of the torch-lit Ma Tara temple. He had been living at the temple grounds for slightly more than a year. He had not yet completed his final initiation into the shakta priesthood, but as the most gifted of the new group of acolytes Harish had extended him the special privilege of entering the inner sanctum with the other priests on this night of the annual festival of Ma Tara puja.

The courtyard was already packed with anxious devotees. Gopala stepped over the broad wooden beam that guarded the diminutive entryway and sat himself down in the lotus position some fifteen feet in front and to the left of the idol.

The dark-blue goddess was no more than four feet in height. She stood triumphantly atop the prone figure of Shiva. Her red tongue lolled lazily from her white mouth, and her four red palms faced menacingly forward. She was dressed in a bright-red silk sari, and her arms were heavily bangled with thick rings of silver. Around her dark neck hung a garland of tightly strung, colorful flowers. In three of her hands were lodged white lotuses, while the top left hand wielded a thick, double-edged sword. Two large white eyes peered out from the encircling sea of blue.

The sanctuary was softly lit by several rows of mounted candles sharply ascending its side and back walls. The dim light was augmented by the smoke of burned chal bark floating freely across the altar and into the rest of the room. The thin haze slightly blurred the goddess' features, thereby adding an eerie quality to the unearthly setting.

Gopala tried to maintain the focus of his attention on the form of the great goddess, but his eyes kept wandering downward to the prostate Shiva who seemed to look up helplessly at his female consort.

One of the pujaris silently approached the altar. He wore a white panjabi cotton shirt, whose sleeves reached almost to his wrists, and the traditional dhoti, which wrapped around his waist, hips, and thighs, leaving his lower legs bare. In his right hand he carried a small brass receptacle that held five burning oil pots. His left hand firmly grasped the top edge of a slightly tarnished brass bell.

When he was directly in front of Ma Tara's image, the priest brought his slow march to a halt and turned toward the goddess. He waved the miniature candelabra in a circular motion. Almost simultaneously he set in motion a rhythmic clanking of the bell. Several devotees who were seated on the outside veranda heard the sound and started beating a large drum.

Gopala watched with the utmost intensity. Another pujari, aided by several assistants, went through the various preparatory steps of the ritual: the blowing of the conch, the fanning of the goddess, the cleaning and clearing of the altar, and the serving to Ma Tara of her evening meal of vegetables, ghi-fried bread, milk, and sweets. All the time the sounds of high pitched devotional songs wafted into the inner sanctum from the courtyard.

After all of the food had been properly consecrated, and Ma Tara had consumed its spiritual essence, numerous pujaris enveloped the altar. Some started decorating the holy shrine with intricately laced strings of jasmine and tuberoses. Others hung an immense white, red, and yellow garland around Ma Tara's neck. Another placed on the altar a moderately-sized, earthen jar filled with water recently taken from the Ganges, surrounding it with shredded pieces of freshly cut coconut. Still others distributed the physical remains of the goddess' dinner to the countless devotees who pressed up impatiently against the side door.

While the worshipers devoured the sacred remains, Harish and his wife, Kamala, approached the altar with heads bowed. Kamala situated herself on the first step, and Harish stood slightly beneath her on the sanctuary floor. The sounds of both Ma Tara and Lord Shiva's names spilled repeatedly from their lips. Gopala watched them sing their devotions, and he instinctively felt that both the goddess and the god whom they were addressing had become mysteriously personified in their figures.

The head pujari had now moved towards the front of the shrine. He seated himself cross-legged on the floor directly in front of Ma Tara's image. Kamala and Harish inconspicuously retreated to the back of the sanctuary, and the noise from the veranda gradually subsided.

The priest's upper body was bare except for a silken yellow cloth, wrapped diagonally around his shoulder and waist, which half-covered his sacred brahmanical thread. A lengthy string of beads hung loosely around his neck, and his forehead displayed a large, pasty, vermilion dot. Two other pujaris, dressed in identical fashion, joined him on either side.

The priest went through the age-old steps of purifying both the shrine and himself for the momentous sacrificial event that was about to take place. While the pujari continued to sporadically chant sacred mantras invoking the goddess' presence, he sipped the water from the earthen jar, made a series of separate offerings to Ma Tara of all the objects on and near the altar, including his own body and mind, and sprinkled saffron-colored rice around the base of the entire shrine.

The pujari stood perfectly still in front of the icon. He remained in silent rapture until he opened his eyes, took a white lotus from the altar and slowly breathed onto it, first through his right nostril and then through his left. He chanted another mantra and placed the flower in one of Ma Tara's blood-red palms.

At the same time that the head priest was making these final preparations, several other pujaris extended two thick ropes from the entryway of the inner sanctum out into the adjacent courtyard. The ropes ran parallel to each other and formed a narrow, corridor-like walkway.

Now that the rituals had almost been completed, four more priests entered the walkway. Each carried a young male goat. As these pujaris brought the animals into the sanctuary, the devotees in the courtyard pushed up against both sides of the ropes, straining to get a better view.

The wildly bleating goats were still dripping with consecrated water from the Ganges. One by one the pujaris arrived at the altar and set down their animals in front of the head priest, who, in turn, quickly marked their foreheads with dabs of vermilion paste To the sound of monotone mantras, he offered the animals up to Ma Tara.

After each goat was consecrated, its accompanying pujari picked the animal back up, raised it to shoulder level, yelled, "Victory to Ma Tara," and ran back down the roped corridor. Unrestrained and ecstatic shouts resounded from the surrounding throng.

Gopala knew their destination: the sacrificial stone. The place was located only a short walking distance from his living quarters, but Gopala had never allowed himself to visit it. Perhaps as a subconscious result of Raychand's reservations, animal sacrifice had remained a stumbling block for him. Even though his attendance at the evening's celebration was a deliberate attempt on his part to overcome these misgivings, his first thought upon noticing the goats' appearance was to get up and leave, to merge anonymously with the crowd and lose himself among them. When a sharp shiver of fear shot through his body, he actually made the first moves in that direction, but something inside him knew that departure was not possible. Harish would be humiliated. So, rather than follow his impulse, Gopala closed his eyes and concentrated with all his might on the mental image of the gleaming goddess.

Within minutes, several servants entered the shrine carrying the goats' severed heads on broad silver platters. Behind them another man, who was short of stature and wore a blood-splattered shirt, stopped at the entryway, raised a dripping red sword high above his head, and fell prostate to the floor. At the moment that his sword hit the ground a chorus of devotees began chanting, "Victory to Ma Tara; Victory to Ma Tara."

The sounds of praise echoed through the sanctuary. The head priest plucked one of the severed heads from the platter. Blood dribbled onto his arms and chest, creating several slow-flowing rivulets. He turned and extended his hands in the direction of Ma Tara. Purplish-red drops sprinkled the altar.

Gopala tried to keep his eyes shut, but he could feel a wedge-like force deep inside his head attempting to pry the orbs open. He gritted his teeth and tightened his facial muscles. The force was too strong; his eyes shot open just as the priest was about to offer the dripping animal's head to the goddess.

The young man tried to look away. He felt like he was falling headlong into some deep dark chasm, but his eyes remained open. Inwardly he could hear himself start to scream, though no noise came from his mouth. His heart beat so quickly and so loudly he was convinced that at any moment the organ would burst open.

He started to feel woozy. Once again he made an effort to look away, but this time his vision was yanked in the direction of Ma Tara's haunting face. Her red, pulsating tongue captured his immediate gaze. His eyes widened even further. He watched the red mass of flesh grow ever larger until it filled up his entire range of vision. The lolling flesh was just about to completely engulf him when seemingly out of nowhere a sudden and inexplicable wave of calm washed slowly through his entire body. He stopped trembling. Everything seemed to stand still.

Later, Gopala had trouble remembering exactly what had taken place during the remainder of the ceremony. Somehow he had managed to make his way with the others to the outside steps of the temple to watch the head priest perform the homa sacrifice by offering clarified butter and flowers into a burning pyre of consecrated wood and then finally dousing the sacred flame with a special mixture of fresh yogurt and water from the Ganges.

Six months later Gopala received his initiation into the shakta priesthood.

Chapter 4

The smoldering funeral pyre sent tiny, thin streams of grey-black smoke spiraling slowly upward into the sky. In the near distance, the murky water of the Ganges flowed quietly on its never-ending journey to the sea. Gopala was sitting close enough to the collapsed pile of ashen wood to feel the energy of the remaining heat, but his body did not experience the sensation. He had been seated at this same spot for more than three hours. His mind had become totally oblivious to the outside world. Even Harish's vehement request that he leave the cremation ground, and continue his mourning at the temple, had produced no effect. The young man was resolutely determined that he would not leave the site until the last embers had died out.

Raychand had died suddenly and unexpectedly. Just three days after participating in the joyous ceremony signaling his nephew's initiation into the Ma Tara priesthood, Raychand had started to feel slightly ill. Several hours later he experienced a severe bout of diarrhea, and by early the next morning his fever had risen to a point where he had become almost delirious. Ayurvedic specialists, hurriedly summoned to his bedside, administered their special herbal concoctions. Meanwhile a number of priests took round-the-clock turns sitting in front of the images of numerous gods on whom they called to bestow upon the sick man their own benevolent healing powers. On several occasions Gopala joined them. Certainly his fervent prayers would be answered.

Raychand did not improve. His temperature continued to rise. He vomited regularly and violently. He lost complete control of his bowels. As a last resort, and against some mild protests from several of the older pujaris, a Western-trained doctor was called to come examine the patient. However, by the time the physician was able to see Raychand, the man was already in the midst of his death throws. According to the doctor, the cause of death was most likely cholera, although he did admit that he found it somewhat strange that no other cases of the deadly disease had recently been reported in the city. As a cautionary measure to ensure that the contagion did not spread, he suggested that the body be cremated as quickly as possible.

The embers continued to smolder. Another two hours passed, and Gopala did not stir from the spot that he had occupied since the completion of the funerary rites. Try as he might, the young man could not empty his head of the images of Raychand's greenish-grey corpse with its foul smelling odor. And whenever he made an effort to concentrate on Ma Tara, it was not the benign mother that he saw but the terrible Tara, her heaving chest bearing a garland of human skulls and her left foot stretched gracefully forward ready to begin her cosmic dance of destruction. These visions did not arouse thoughts of fear. Rather, his mind was occupied by an intense feeling of unbounded and universal sorrow mixed with an almost nauseating sense of nihilistic disgust.

Pain and suffering were not new to Gopala; he had known bitter grief when his father had died years before, but this was of an altogether different quality. Not only was his beloved uncle gone, his flesh reduced to a mere handful of smoldering ashes, but the entire world appeared to him as nothing more than one gigantic, rotting carcass.

The embers finally cooled to the point where he could touch them. Gopala arose and walked mechanically up to the pyre. He could clearly see Raychand's charred skull and bones. He knelt down and placed his shaking hand next to the remains. He covered his fingers with some of the surrounding ash. In a gesture more automatic than calculated, he raised his fingers upward and roughly smeared the warm grey powder across his forehead. He remained on his knees unable to turn away from the haunting black skull. Its eyes seemed to stare straight back at him, their hollow sockets reaffirming that death was indeed lord.

A soft hand on his left shoulder jarred the young man from his reflective trance. He looked up to see the face of Harish. "Come Gopala," the temple owner said. "It is time for you to depart from this place. I have brought my coach. We can return tomorrow to collect Raychand's remains."

Gopala still did not want to leave, but this time his resistance was less firm. After a bit more coaxing from Harish, he finally gave in. Silently he chanted "Om Krim Tara." He got up, took one last look at the pyre and followed the man across the deserted cremation ground. At the top of a small incline stood Harish's carriage.

"I think it best for your well-being that you come and stay at my residence," Harish emphatically declared once the carriage had started to move away from the cremation ground. "As I am sure you know, there is too much commotion in the priests' quarters. What you need for the time being is some peace and quiet. There is a spare room downstairs, which can be easily transformed for your needs."

For the first time since Raychand had fallen ill, Gopala could feel a trickle of warmth within himself. He tenderly leaned his head against Harish's broad shoulder. "Thank you so much Harish Babu," he whispered. "You are so good to me."

Gopala's new home was the same two-story wooden structure where he and his uncle had first met Harish. After Gopala had become a permanent resident at the temple, both men had on separate occasions been personally invited to the building's parlor to converse with the temple owner, and thus his occupation of a small room just off this same parlor did not evoke in Gopala the sense of an alien environment. Indeed, compared to the tightly cramped priests' quarters, the mansion had an air of security and safety about it which at times rekindled Gopala's distant memories of Ishakpur.

Even though the house provided a calm atmosphere, Gopala continued to remain troubled. Life seemed tasteless and empty. On most days he could barely bring himself to go to the temple and make his offerings to Ma Tara. The only relief from the almost pervasive feeling of despair came when he was able to be alone with Harish in the temple's extensive flower gardens. There, and there alone, whatever joy remained within him was able to show its face. At those times it was as if he were magically back in Ishakpur frivolously playing with Ram Das. In those beautiful gardens, brief glimpses of the world of lila, which had almost been extinguished from his life since coming to the city, temporarily reappeared, only to vanish when he and Harish had to depart.

Late in the evening of the one-month anniversary of Raychand's death, Gopala lay restlessly on his cot. For much of the night he had been turning this way and that, trying to find a position in which he could get comfortable enough to fall asleep. The air coming in from the opened shutter was warm and moist. Tiny beads of perspiration gathered on his skin. Slowly his consciousness softened, yet he could not completely let go. He could only drift slowly in and out of sleep.

In this dream-like haze Gopala subconsciously began imagining himself in the form of a stray and inured dog, longingly roaming Ishakpur's dark, empty lanes in search of Ram Das. He had just exited one such lane and entered into a grassy, sunlit meadow. Unexpectedly he heard a beautiful voice. He magically abandoned his limp and ran joyfully in the direction of an old, bent-over tree. Instantly a young boy appeared from behind the tree's gnarled trunk. Atop his body, however, was not the smiling, friendly face of his young companion but Raychand's cracked and charred skull.

Gopala's body began to tremble, and he sat up in a fright.

He gasped violently for air. He could only think of one thing: going to Harish. *But what would the owner think? How would he explain his nightmare?* He lay back down, concentrated on taking several deep breaths, and then shut his eyes. He firmly rubbed his closed eyelids and forehead with his hands, trying desperately to relieve the stress. The pangs of anxiety did not yield. Instead, they grew more intense. Breathing became unbearably difficult. He felt as if he were going to drown.

Gopala pushed himself back up to a sitting position. He knew that Kamala had gone to Calcutta several days earlier to spend an extended period of time with her parents, so he would not be intruding on man and wife . . . He decided it would be all right.

Harish's sleeping quarters were located on the building's second floor, just to the right of the spot where the spiral staircase met the upper landing. Gopala left his room, tiptoed his way across the parlor floor and up the winding staircase. The last thing he wanted to do was wake one of the servants. He reached the top of the steps and could see that Harish's bedroom door had been left slightly ajar. He continued forward until he was within arms distance of his destination and then stopped. He hesitated. Doubts raced through his head. *Am I doing the right thing? What if Harish becomes angry? Perhaps I should return to my room?* . . . He weakly pushed the heavy slab of wood forward, creating a space of several inches. After one final hesitation, he put his mouth up to the crack. "Harish," he whispered.

He waited for a reply but heard nothing. The thought that there was still time to leave crossed his mind. No, he must speak to Harish. Once more he whispered, this time more forcefully. "It is Gopala. I need to see you."

Still there was no reply. Gopala's mind raced . . .*If I must I will wake him he decided.*

The young priest cautiously pushed the door wide open and entered the room. He looked around. There was no sign of Harish. *Where could he be?* A feeling of abandonment briefly came over Gopala before he recognized the absurdity of such an emotion.

Harish owes me nothing, he said to himself as he swiftly turned and departed.

Back in his own room Gopala chided himself for his stupidity, but beneath the anger lay a momentous insight. He realized that he really was alone. If anyone could help him, it was not Harish. Only the goddess herself could save him now.

Chapter 5

I am extremely worried about the young man," said Harish. "I know it is not unusual when a boy loses a close male relative for him to experience a deep sense of loss, and to expresses it through an extended period of mourning. But it has been well over six months now since Raychand died, yet Gopala continues having these episodes. Some last up to several days. At such times, he will hardly eat or sleep, and even more disturbing are some of the very strange things he does."

The man to whom Harish was speaking was his brother-in-law, Manindra Gupta. Manindra was not directly involved in the religious affairs of the Ma Tara temple, but he was well-connected both socially and politically, and he had his sights fixed on making Harish's monument of devotion to the goddess the focal point of a resurgent Hindu nationalism in Benares.

Though he was known for his voracious appetite, both for food and women, in contrast to Harish's heavy frame and thick build, Manindra's body was on the thin side. His face was dominated by a strong jaw and forehead. He chin was cleanly shaven. Above his upper lip sat a neatly manicured mustache. His thick black hair was starting to overlap both of his ears. Like his brother-in-law, he was attired in a silk coat and pajama pants.

"When you say 'strange,' Harish Babu, could you please

explain just exactly what you mean," Manindra demanded. "Strange to you and me, or strange to those bizarre creatures that inhabit the world of religious incredulities?"

Manindra took some roasted nuts from one of the condiment dishes sitting in a neat row atop an elegantly etched glass table and tossed them into his betel-stained mouth.

Harish knew that Manindra was once again displaying the cynical side of his personality. The evidence was found in the grin that now manifested itself on his brother-in-law's face. Harish acted, however, as if he did not notice the posturing.

"Now and again Gopala seems to completely lose his sense of reality," the temple owner replied in a dry voice. "At these times he rolls helplessly on the ground, plastering himself with mud, or he weeps uncontrollably and calls out for Ma Tara to show herself to him. On two occasions he has been found back at the cremation grounds covered in excrement and babbling incomprehensibly."

"I must say that there are times when I just do not understand you, Harish Babu. Why on earth do you concern yourself with this country boy? You have absolutely no responsibility towards him. He probably needs his mother, or better yet, a hungry wife."

For a second time a wicked smile lit up Manindra's face. "If you really want my advice, I think you should send him back to his village . . . and the sooner, the better. Your valuable time should not be spent having to deal with such childish nonsense. The temple has many needs. It is starting to become known throughout the region, and it requires your full attention."

Harish also took some of the condiments. He munched a hand full of dry, spicy noodles and reflected on Manindra's words. "Unlike myself, my dear Manindra, you are an extremely practical man . . . might I even say, a true man of the world. I respect this aspect of your character, but to be honest with you, I am not as practical as you are. The fact of the matter is, that I have become quite fond of the boy."

Manindra shook his head.

"But do not get me wrong, my dear brother-in-law, there

is much more to the situation than simple personal affection. I have spent quite a bit of time with Gopala recently, and I can perceive in him great spiritual potential. He has a unique dynamism of spirit, a certain depth of perception that far outstrips any of the pujaris who are currently residing here at the temple."

"A unique dynamism of spirit," Manindra repeated, "like rolling around at the cremation grounds covered in excrement?"

"Believe me, I know there are some problems, Manindra Babu," Harish quickly countered. "And that is one reason why I speak to you so bluntly here today. But, and I know that this may sound incredible to your ears, I am convinced there is much more here than meets the eye. You see, I have a sense that in some mysterious way these episodes of his are manifestations of titanic internal spiritual struggles. Gopala's soul has . . . it has become a battlefield where both gods and demons are vying for control. If the boy can emerge from this conflict victorious, there will be virtually no limit to the powers of which he will be capable."

Manindra had another sarcastic remark on the tip of his tongue but thought better of using it. "And if not?" he merely asked.

"Of course the entire situation is in Ma Tara's hands," said Harish. "But I do remember well what the goddess revealed to me that night years ago. She spoke about the future eminence of this temple, and how a special young man would take up the reins of leadership."

Harish reached down and scooped up some of the roasted nuts but did not take them to his mouth. "And while you might not believe in my own religious incredulities," he continued, stressing the last word while looking straight into Manindra's eyes, "there is one thing I do know: the Ma Tara temple will never become renowned without the presence of a great soul to guide it."

"So what will you do?"

"Actually it is quite simple; I will be patient. I will simply wait and make sure that no harm comes to him."

Harish turned and walked lazily out onto the sun-filled veranda. Manindra followed him, sensing that his brother-in-law was not yet finished with the discussion. "But I do need to ask a small favor of you," Harish said once Manindra had reached his side. "I have just found out that I must go to Calcutta for several days on temple business, and I would greatly appreciate it if you and Rohilla would stay here in the house during that time so you can keep an eye on Gopala."

Manindra grimaced, and Harish was quick to notice the facial change. "Do not worry, Manindra Babu," he said, putting his large right arm around the smaller man's shoulder. "You will not have to watch over him twenty-four hours a day. The other pujaris know how to deal with his episodes. I would like to make sure, however, that Gopala does not try and leave the temple grounds, and for this reason I would feel much better knowing you were here. And what is more, you and your lovely wife can keep my precious Kamala entertained." It was now Harish's turn to smile.

Manindra more than understood the reference to the sisters' incompatibility. "And what does Kamala think of this idea?" he questioned.

Kamala is a good Hindu wife," Harish said briskly. "She will go along with whatever decision I make."

"Of course, I will provide you with any assistance you might need Harish Babu," Manindra responded. "And it goes without saying that I wouldn't want Ma Tara's chosen one to go astray, now would I?"

Harish did not bother to look at the expression he knew was blanketing Manindra's face. "Thank you so much, Manindra. I knew that I could count on you. Now, are you feeling hungry? The servants have just brought some wonderful new melons from the market. Come, let us test them."

A brazen orange sun slowly lowered itself into the horizon. Gopala sat motionless on the bottom step of the temple's bathing ghats. Periodically, water lapped onto his bare legs, but he paid the wet beads of moisture no attention. The only movement from his entire body came from his lips, which were busy pouring forth a series of almost soundless murmurings. His face and body were covered with dirt and ash, and in his hands he held the drying and crumbling remains of dog excrement. A handful of devotees making their final ablutions of the day periodically glanced in his direction, some out of plain curiosity, some out of anxious discomfort, and some out of religious awe. Several thought he must be mad. Others faithfully surmised that these were signs of a great saint.

Without any signs of warning, Gopala's random mumbling turned into a shrill and distinct cry: "Yet another day has passed, Ma Tara, and still you do not reveal yourself to me? What kind of mother are you who would abandon her own child like this?"

Gopala fully extended himself on the water strewn step and rubbed his forehead forcefully against the stone. "You showed yourself to Harish Babu. Why will you not make yourself known to me?"

He began to weep. The tears soon joined forces with the trickle of blood that made its way down the front of his head and onto the bridge of his nose.

Many of the bathers began to leave the water in fear.

"Where are you all going?" exclaimed one of the temple pujaris who was bathing amongst them. "Why do you flee in the manner of frightened sheep? This young man is harmless. He is only crying out for that which we all desire. You have all heard of, and even praised, the devoted gopis of Braj who longed for union with their beloved Krishna more than life itself, and yet when you see this same passionate desire being expressed before your very eyes, what do you do? You get up and run away."

When they heard the older pujari's lament, several of the people stopped and returned to complete their religious duties. Yet despite the priest's admonishment, most of the worshipers left the water and sped rapidly up the steep steps, all the while busily whispering their thoughts to one another.

"Are you real, Ma," Gopala called out yet again, "or are all the tales about your miraculous powers only false stories made up by treacherous poets in order to fool the people? Is the image in your temple just a piece of profane rock? If you really do exist and are not just a figment of people's vain imaginings, then why is it that you don't answer me when I call to you? Are you so vain?"

The shadows lengthened. Gopala continued to direct his rantings towards the goddess, sometimes pleading with her, sometimes cajoling her, sometimes regaling her. One by one, the remaining bathers exited the water until only the two pujaris remained at the river's edge.

"Gopala, I have finished my ablutions and am going back to the temple," the other pujari announced. "I think it wise that you do the same and come with me. Remember, no one can control Ma Tara's will. Any attempt to do so is a hopeless task. The best that anyone can do is put their complete confidence in the goddess. You demand proof, but such proof does not require any trust."

Gopala looked over at the older man. The eyes through which he peered were bloodshot. His facial features were contorted. "What kind of mother requires so much?" he pleaded. "What kind of mother requires the sacrifice of her own son's head? Am I no better than a helpless goat?"

Perhaps he really is mad after all, the older pujari thought to himself. *He is making no sense whatsoever*. The man attempted no answer but silently ascended the steps in long powerful strides.

Gopala's eyes followed him. "Does she want my head?" he again cried out

The pujari stopped and turned. "If I were you, Gopala, I would not stay down there too long. Manindra is certain to get worried and send someone to retrieve you."

The pujari looked to see if his words had registered with the young man. It appeared that they had not. He spun back around and returned to his climb.

Gopala recommenced his lamentations. He maintained his periodic tirade until close to midnight. Then he eventually became quiet.

It was pitch dark. The moon had not yet made its appearance. His thoughts turned back to his earlier words, and he instantaneously found himself reliving the events of the night of the Ma Tara puja, except that this time it was not the goat's blood-dripping head that the priest held tightly in his grasp. It was his own heavily scarred and mutilated head. And just as on that evening he had felt a compelling force deep within him taking over his will, he once again found himself ensnared by a similar power. This time it was pulling him to his feet, drawing him up the steps and across the temple's courtyard towards Ma Tara's inner sanctuary. His gait was sure and steady, his pace quick.

Gopala entered the sanctuary and approached the shrine without any of the usual displays of obeisance. The room was empty of all people. He and the goddess were alone, standing face to face. He stared at her mask-like eyes. "If this is what you wish for your child, then I will become your goat," he shouted, and he stepped onto the altar.

Just as his flesh made contact with the cold stone, he felt an indescribable surge of energy infuse his entire body. He staggered backwards. He could see nothing; all became black. But a voice, as clear and as distinct as any he had ever heard, sounded in his ears: "I am in everything; Everything is in me."

Chapter 6

Manindra entered the parlor and carefully adjusted his freshly ironed silk turban. "You are to be congratulated, Harish Babu," he said. "Once again you have proven yourself to be a man of tremendous insight. Throughout the entire city, people cannot stop talking about the mystical powers of the young priest, Gopala. In nearly every bazaar and neighborhood the story is the same."

"Well I cannot take all the credit, my dear Manindra. After all, it was during your stay here that the goddess appeared to Gopala. A wise man might conclude that it was actually you who brought us such good fortune."

Both men laughed heartily.

"No Harish Babu. I must honestly say that I cannot take the least bit of credit for any of these things. As you well know, when it comes to belief in epiphanies, I am at best a skeptic. In fact, if there were any religious bones in this aging body of mine, they would certainly be said to side with the nirgun philosophers. An Absolute without qualities and beyond time and space I can accept, if not completely understand; a personal god or goddess who reveals its will to certain men . . . well, let us just say that such an idea plays havoc with my intellect."

"Make sure you don't let your wife hear you say such things," Harish chided. "From what Kamala tells me her sister is a very devout bhakta, and she wishes her husband were the same."

Again both men laughed.

A servant carrying an enormous silver tray adorned with a blue and white porcelain teapot and matching cups and saucers appeared in the doorway. "Come, Manindra. Let us sit outside and take our tea on the veranda," Harish suggested. "The weather is so marvelous; it is a crime to stay inside."

"I could not agree with you more, Harish Babu. The cool breeze outside is absolutely delightful."

The servant followed the men on to the the veranda and poured the tea. When he had completed his task and returned to the house, the temple owner promptly turned to the matter which lay at the heart of Manindra's visit. "So, my dear brother, what news have you heard from your contacts? Are these men prepared to support the temple now that we have a budding saint?"

Manindra took a long, slow sip of the sweet, milky tea and then returned the cup to his lap. "I can tell you this, Harish Babu, they are without doubt very much impressed with Gopala. The young man's charismatic personality and superior meditative powers cannot be questioned. And, as I mentioned to you a few moments ago, they are unquestionably aware of how swiftly his fame is spreading, even beyond Benares, but . . . "

"But," said Harish, "It seems as if there is always a 'but' with these men." He put his cup down firmly on a nearby table and rose to his feet. "Why can't they just accept the boy's powers for what they are?" The last words left his mouth at the level of a shout.

"Please try and remain calm, Harish Babu." Manindra's response expressed his growing irritation at his brother-in-law's reaction. "Sit down, and I will do my best to explain the substance of their concerns."

Harish thought seriously about sending Manindra back to his acquaintances with a fitting answer to their bothersome questions, but at the last moment his good sense prevailed, and he calmly sat back down in the chair to hear his relative's explanation.

"You must remember, Harish Babu, that these men come

primarily from intellectual and martial backgrounds. They
have all been raised and educated in the traditional Hindu virtues, and consequently when they hear secondhand stories
about Gopala's dressing up and worshiping in the guise of a
female, well . . . to be quite frank, they become, how might I
put it, . . . somewhat squeamish."

"You say these men are knowledgeable Hindus," returned
Harish. "Do they not know that many of our greatest saints
have worshipped in such a manner? Have they forgotten about
the renowned Bengali acharya Chaitanya? Or are they not
aware that he became famous precisely because of his passionate love for Krishna, which he demonstrated by taking the role
of Krishna's divine consort, Radha?"

"I cannot contest what you are saying, Harish," Manindra
acknowledged, "but, you must understand what I am trying to
tell you. These men are interested in supporting a Hinduism
that represents strength and virility, a Hinduism that can stand
on an equal footing with either Christianity or Islam. They
have absolutely no problem offering their allegiance to the
goddess Tara, but it is a goddess of power to whom they will
give their support, not a goddess of divine frolic."

Harish was quick with his rejoinder. "But are you not for-
getting something of great consequence, Manindra? Are you
not leaving out the important fact that Ma Tara revealed herself to Gopala, and it is therefore not proper for us mere mortals to try and manipulate the will of the goddess?"

"Now, Harish Babu, you know just as well as I do that the
divine will is not so easily understood . . . that there are indeed
an infinite number of perspectives from which it can be perceived . . . Unless, of course, you would have me believe
that you are claiming Gopala is an avatar—Ma Tara's own
incarnation?"

Harish could see that Manindra was trying to drive him
into a corner. "All I know is what Gopala told me of the event,"
he answered.

"Which was?"

Harish cleared this throat. "He claimed that he was
blessed with a direct and immediate vision of Ma Tara. That

this experience . . ." Harish paused to search for the exact words he wanted, "that this experience could only be described as an intensely concentrated stream of bliss from which it became clearly known to him that he was to worship the goddess in the manner of the great Hindu heroes and heroines of the past as reported in the holy scriptures. That is, he was to worship her as being ever-present in all things."

Manindra slapped the table lightly with his right hand and looked directly at his host. His eyes revealed a new enthusiasm "In that case, it should present no real problem. As there are certainly numerous heroes and heroines in the Hindu holy books who can be identified with intelligence, courage, and manly valor, and who worshipped their gods and goddesses as manifestations of these same virtues, it should be easy enough for you to encourage the young priest to emphasize these sacred paths in his own teachings. In other words, Harish Babu, you must make him see that what India needs at this moment in her history is not another Chaitanya, but another Shivaji, a vital spirit who understands what it really means to say that Ma Tara is the great mother of Hinduism, a man who would not only see the goddess as being present in all things, but who would protect his homeland from the condescending attacks of the foreigner with his clarity of thought and powers of self-control."

Manindra left his chair and started pacing back and forth along the front of the veranda. "If we cannot conquer the malicious foreigner by the force of our arms," he asserted, "then we must conquer him by the power of our ideas. Yes, intellectual and spiritual virility, that is what we need."

"It would seem that you are the one who needs to calm down now," Harish said as he watched his brother-in law's emotions rise. "You sound very much like one of those 'India for the Indians' fellows."

Manindra could feel the muscles tighten in his neck. "Well, let me put it this way, Harish Babu. I have not forgotten the events of 1857 and the patriotic warriors who opposed the British, and neither have these men." He had not lowered his voice.

Harish allowed Manindra time to calm himself. He reached casually for the teapot and slowly poured its contents into his empty cup. He let it sit for a few more moments and then raised the vessel to his lips and took another sip.

"What you ask will not be so easy to accomplish," he said after putting his cup down. "What attracts most people to Gopala is not his knowledge, but his devotional intensity and the ecstatic trance states that such devotion is able to engender. This type of spiritual passion cannot be orchestrated. It comes to him uncontrollably from within, one might even say naturally."

"Then let me make a suggestion, Harish Babu." Manindra had returned to a state of emotional equilibrium. "Find someone who can teach Gopala the truth of the spiritual path of Vedanta. I know that he is a bright young man, and he will no doubt respect the ancient wisdom. And what is more, such knowledge will undoubtedly help bring some balance to his emotional displays. As everyone knows, the greatest masters perfect all three paths: knowledge, devotion, and action."

Finally, one of Manindra's ideas had struck a chord with Harish. "Your suggestion makes a great deal of sense," he said. "Knowledge of all the spiritual disciplines is certainly a worthy pursuit. I will do what I can to find such a teacher for Gopala."

Manindra's eyes lit up and his face softened. "You will not regret your decision, Harish Babu. Under your guidance I am sure that Gopala can bring to this temple the support you seek. Now I must take my leave. Rohilla and I are entertaining guests tonight. And, I might add, several of these guests will certainly be interested in what we have said here today."

Harish stood up and went swiftly to Manindra's side. The men firmly embraced. "I appreciate your support and good advice," he whispered. "And let me assure you that your friends will not be disappointed."

Harish and Manindra separated. They walked briskly into the house and through the parlor to the foyer. "I will contact you soon," Harish said while waiting for the servant to open the door for his guest.

"Oh, and one other thing, Harish Babu." Manindra

stopped his descent down the stairs. "It would be helpful if Gopala were married. You know . . . a display of Hindu virility."

Manindra did not bother to wait for Harish's reply. He hurriedly spun back around and stepped stridently toward his awaiting carriage.

The light from a radiant full moon filtered gently into Gopala's darkened room through the half-open wooden shutters, giving the statue of the flute-playing Krishna its only luminescence. The small stone image stood next to figures of several other deities, all of whom flanked the larger icon of Ma Tara.

Gopala stared longingly at the blue-skinned shepherd god whose tilted head, cocked waist, and bent knee were now the object of his adoration. "You are so fickle, my sweet lord," he uttered in a soft, undulating voice. "Tell me, why is it that you only give me a sideways glance and never look directly into my eyes? Why do you tease your loyal devotees so? And why is it that just when you seem to be on the verge of fulfilling our desires you so cunningly run off? Where are you going? I know you will not answer, but tonight I will not let you go until you dance with me. Tonight we will dance the ras lila together."

Gopala seductively raised his heavily bangled arms into the air and began slowly waving them back and forth in front of the image. His feet slid along the floor, first in one direction and then in the other. The yellow and purple silk sari that adorned his sleek body seemed to follow their movement, swaying in rhythmic unison with each slide step that he made.

In the midst of his beguiling dance, Gopala's words unaccountably turned into song. "Separation from you, O my beloved, makes this world a mere empty shell. When you remain aloof, these eyes of mine become forever restless. O love of my life, when will you come and dance with your faithful servant? If he does not dance with you tonight, his heart will undoubtedly be left unfulfilled."

Gopala started slowly turning as he moved. His gyrating hands remained above his head, mirroring the motion of his swaying hips. He stopped singing and once again addressed the icon in normal speech. "You cannot fool me, my sweet Krishna, for you see, I know who you really are. Your flute is Ma's sword, and your song is her melody. Come dance with me Ma Tara; come dance with me."

Gopala prolonged his dance, unaware that he was being watched. Standing in the open doorway was Harish who had become enchanted by the young priest's enticing movement and could say nothing. *How wonderful he looks*, he thought to himself. *His energy is pure delight.*

Eventually Gopala sensed the eyes upon him. He looked towards the doorway. "Good evening Harish Babu," he said. He lowered his arms and brought the movement of his feet to a sudden halt.

Harish regained his composure and took several steps towards Gopala. "My carriage is waiting," he said. He calmly placed his large hand behind Gopala's head. "The Ganges is exquisite tonight."

Gopala understood that Harish's comment was meant to be more than a suggestion. "Right now . . . like this?" he asked.

Harish nodded, and the two men quietly departed the house and entered the covered carriage.

During their entire outward journey neither man spoke. It was not until the driver pulled off the bumpy roadway onto an isolated bluff overlooking the river and brought the carriage to a complete halt that Harish's voice ruptured the stillness.

"Gopala," he said, "I would like to ask a special favor of you." He stared directly into the young man's heavily shadowed eyes

Gopala did not know what to say.

"There is a very wise man whom I would like you to meet. He has studied for many years with some of the most famous gurus and learned acharyas in Benares. His knowledge of the holy texts is impeccable, and, more importantly, he has mastered the profound truths of the advaita philosophy of the unity of existence. I feel strongly that you could learn a great deal from him."

"Of course, Harish Babu," Gopala answered. "I am always willing to learn from those who think they can explain Ma Tara's innermost secrets."

Harish understood well the irony behind Gopala's blunt expression. "Well, good then, that issue is settled. I will arrange for him to come to the temple as soon as possible . . . Oh, and there is just one other thing, Gopala."

Harish hesitated. For a brief moment he thought that perhaps he should wait for another time and place to reveal his next request, but he quickly decided against any delay. "I have received news from your uncle in Ishakpur," he abruptly said. "Your mother very much wants for you to be married . . . and I support her wish."

Gopala's head jutted slightly forward. His eyes became large and his lower lip dropped. "You know that is impossible," he stuttered.

Harish immediately regretted his decision and changed the topic. "Tonight the full moon shining on the water is something truly marvelous to behold," he said. "Come, Gopala, we must walk. We can talk about your mother's marital wishes later."

The temple owner threw open the carriage door, stepped briskly out into the night and beckoned Gopala to follow him.

Later that night when Gopala was alone in his room, he approached the tarnished brass statue of Rama that stood next to the image of Krishna. "I have returned, O my Lord," he reverently whispered. "Your Sita has been enticed by Ravana, but she has remained faithful to you. Only you know the contents of my heart. They want to steal me from you, but only in the illusory world of maya will their schemes appear successful. I will always be yours."

The tears that flowed from Gopala's eyes turned the dark shadow which lined them into black smudge. "I will always be yours," he repeated; "I will always be yours."

Chapter 7

The aging white horse ambled casually down the dusty dirt road that led to the heart of the village. Across its stringy, greyish mane lay several large garlands of red and orange flowers. On both sides of the animal, shouts of intermittent revelry filled the air as the celebrants slowly and methodically accompanied the tired beast and its youthful rider towards the recently constructed marriage pavilion.

From his position perched well above the noisy crowd, Gopala could clearly eye the structure's canvas roof and its numerous colorful flags flitting playfully in the late afternoon breeze. His massive cream-colored turban, laced with ever-so-fine threads of gold brocade, and his buttonless white jacket gave him a regal appearance, but the stolid lines on his face and the stiffness with which he held his head indicated a striking lack of joy.

In the small room adjacent to the pavilion, the young bride anxiously awaited the arrival of the groom. Chandramani was similarly surrounded by family members and friends with whom she nervously shared small talk. Her red and gold bridal sari hung loosely over her petite but well-formed body. Her matching head shawl was delicately draped to one side of her handsome face.

She had never met, nor even seen, her husband-to-be, but rumors of his sometimes strange behavior had filtered through to her by way of the intricate network of pujari gossip mongers. Despite the continual reassurance by Chandramani's mother that the young man from the nearby village to whom she had been pledged was an excellent match, the bride could not rid herself of ever-mounting feelings of intense anxiety.

When the groom's party finally reached their destination, Gopala was helped down from the horse by his uncle. "This is indeed an auspicious and joyful day for the entire family," he boomed. "You have made your mother extremely happy. May the Supreme Lord shower you and your new bride with his eternal blessings."

The older man bent down and gently touched his nephew's feet.

Gopala heard his uncle's joyous words of praise, but he remained completely unmoved by them. He had not wanted the marriage; he had consented to it only to please others. Indeed, it was not until he had been completely convinced that Ma Tara approved of the union that his decision became final. One thing was certain in his mind: the marriage would never be consummated.

Gopala's mother and aunt stood together several feet away from the groom. His mother was leaning in the direction of her sister who had only arrived that very morning from Calcutta. "I never thought this day would come. And you must admit that Gopala certainly looks handsome."

"Yes he is a handsome young man," the woman confirmed. "But what about the bride? Does she do him justice?"

"We probably could have held out for better, but the rumor mongers hurt us," Gopala's mother answered. "As you will see, she is not the most unattractive girl in the world, and in spite of her size she is strong, so I am certain she will produce many healthy children."

The bride's mother and father stood at the entrance to the pavilion and awaited their new son-in-law's arrival. Gopala, however, was in no mood to rush forward. He lingered motionless next to the horse where he continued to chat with a number of his close relatives. Only after he was prodded by his mother's severe stare did the reluctant groom eventually end his conversation and approach his new in-laws. Even then, he refused to make eye contact with them. Instead, he ungraciously snatched the freshly cut tree branch offered him by Chandramani's mother, proffered a hurried and formal bow, and curtly marched directly into the pavilion. In a similar manner, he stoically accepted several garlands from well-wishers, all the while maintaining the most serious of poses.

It was now time for Chandramani to make her entrance. She carried in her arms two huge garlands of pink, white, and yellow flowers, one to place around Gopala's neck, and the other to present him for her own garlanding. But her thoughts were not centered on this aspect of the ritual. Instead she kept thinking about her husband's physical appearance. *Would he be handsome like her mother had promised, or had this just been a carrot to lead her happily forward into the union? What if he were unattractive or misshapen?*

She passed through the doorway and into the pavilion. Her apprehension built to a crescendo, and the feeling of relief that she felt upon finally encountering Gopala made her somewhat woozy. But she kept her composure and walked calmly towards him as if she had never given the situation a second thought.

As for Gopala, he had no concern whatsoever about his bride's physical attributes. When he saw her fair complexion, her delicate, well-balanced features, and her large brown eyes, he passed no judgment. He simply lowered his head in a mechanical fashion and prepared himself to receive his garland. Moreover, once the flowers had been draped comfortably around his neck, he sullenly completed the rite by nonchalantly placing the second garland in its required location across Chandramani's shoulders.

The event continued in its traditional fashion, the same way Hindu weddings had unfolded in this region for countless decades. The bride and groom received their relatives and guests; the entire wedding party dined together; and the priests initiated the ceremony by reciting copious passages from the Vedas. This was followed by a seemingly endless series of ritual offerings, each accompanied by a special sacred verse.

When the puja offerings were finally over, the couple

circled the sacred fire seven times. Chandramani led the first four circumambulations and Gopala the last three.

Some two hours after the wedding's commencement, the groom placed a smudgy streak of red powder in the part of his new wife's hair. It was at this point Gopala almost reneged on his commitment. For some reason the red powder reminded him of the blood spilling forth from the young goat's severed head at the Ma Tara Puja, and he was momentarily repulsed by the terrifying thought of his own sacrifice at the altar of conventionality. Only a quick glance in the direction of Harish, who was slowly nodding his head in agreement, and the memory that Ma Tara had herself sanctified the marital arrangement, allowed him to finish the deed and thereby bring the ceremony to its proper conclusion.

Later that evening when the celebration had been completed and Gopala had left Chandramani in her village to spend one last night with her parents and siblings, he kept his prearranged rendezvous with Ram Das. The two young men met in a grove of trees near Ishakpur's southern edge where years before as boys they had created and acted out countless stories based on the exploits of gods, goddesses, and demons. Much to Gopala's disappointment, the short conversation made it readily apparent that Ram Das had changed. While his old friend could still speak fondly of those past times, he also made it very clear that he saw them only as childish memories. He was much more interested in hearing about the size of Gopala's dowry and discussing his own plans for marriage and worldly wealth than recalling the stories found in the Epics or the Puranas.

By the time the sun had risen the next morning Gopala had already come to the conclusion that within the week he would return to Benares. Both his mother and new bride's pleas that he spend more time in Ishakpur were ignored. Chandramani could follow him at a later date if she wished, but he would under no circumstances allow his marriage to keep him away from the city for an extended period. In making his decision he was doing more than just ridding himself of a domineering parent and two overly-protective in-laws. During the first few days of his stay in Ishakpur, he had thought that perhaps there was still some possibility his life might find a source of rejuvenated meaning within its confines. After meeting with Ram Das, he now knew for certain that village life, with all its nostalgic associations, was truly dead for him, and that his future, along with whatever uncertainty it might hold, lay totally and completely with Harish and the Ma Tara temple.

*

Chapter 8

Nine months had passed since Gopala left Ishakpur and returned to Benares. Although Chandramani had not wanted to leave the countryside, her father was adamant that a new wife belonged at her husband's side. And so, despite his daughter's numerous tears and lamentations, he ordered her to accompany Gopala back to the sacred city.

As his wedding gift to the couple, Harish arranged for Gopala and Chandramani to occupy their own private living quarters. The two-room, plaster-walled structure he assigned them was located near the very heart of the temple compound, approximately halfway between the main sanctuary and the bathing ghats. The small house was bordered on three sides by high, ivy-draped stone walls, which protected the new residents from the potential inquisitive glances of both devotees and pilgrims.

Within the dwelling's dark and narrow confines, Chandramani came to realize that the life her parents had enthusiastically promised her in return for their daughter's marital cooperation was never going to be fulfilled. Gopala was rarely at the house during daylight hours, and since it was considered immoral for a woman of her caste and stature to be out in public by herself, most of her days were spent entirely alone. In line with Gopala's vow, she soon came to know that she would never have any children. At the tender age of eighteen, Chandramani had become a virtual widow.

Just as Harish had promised, upon returning to the temple Gopala was provided with a Vedantic teacher. Krishnadas came from a long and very distinguished line of textual scholars. He had been trained from youth by the best linguists throughout northern India and was said to have committed to memory by an early age not only the entire *Rig Veda*, but several of the most prominent Upanishads.

Five years earlier, when he had just turned thirty-five, Krishnadas had quite abruptly abandoned the life of the scholar and taken initiation as a sannyasin. In so doing he had departed Benares for a small hermitage in the foothills of the Himalayas where, rather than writing commentaries on the sacred texts, he sought to actuate by means of intense meditation the spiritual insights contained within their verses. His aged father had been a close friend of Kamala's grandfather, and it was in response to a paternal request, brokered by Harish through Kamala's father, that Krishnadas had agreed to tutor the young priest in the fundamentals of the philosophy of divine unity.

The two men met every other morning in a small meditation hut situated in the far corner of a tree-lined grove a short distance from Gopala's new residence. On those days that he saw Krishnadas, Gopala would awaken several hours before the sun rose, go to the bathing ghats to perform his ritual ablutions, attended to Ma Tara's morning needs, and then depart the temple for his lesson.

The teacher would always greet his student in the same manner. As Gopala entered the hut, the naked sanyasin would remain in the lotus position with his eyes gently shut. Once the young man had seated himself on the woven hemp mat laying directly across from him, the guru would slowly open his eyes, stare penetratingly at the middle of his student's forehead, and then purposefully reach down into a small container filled with vermilion paste, and vigorously stir the contents with his finger. When this finger was adequately covered with the paste, Krishnadas would reach across and forcefully apply it to the very spot on Gopala's forehead that his eyes had previously marked as their target. Then in a commanding voice he would ask Gopala a question.

One morning several months into his course of instruction, Gopala arrived at the meditation hut a little later than usual and hurriedly sat down on the mat in front of Krishnadas. He was anticipating a reprimand. The teacher, however, said nothing about his student's tardiness and proceeded to perform his normal preparatory ritual. But this time instead of asking Gopala a question, he closed his eyes and for an extended period of time whispered sacred verses. Gopala did not pay attention to their content but rather focused is eyes on a stone lingam sitting next to the guru.

"Is this lingam real?" Krishnadas unexpectedly asked. His eyes flew open.

The outburst startled Gopala. He became disoriented. His thoughts flashed back to those warm summer days on the outskirts of Ishakpur and his clandestine encounters with the naked sadhus. The feelings associated with these memories both repelled and attracted him. He soon began to experience the onset of that old state of mental confusion, which since the day he had been graced by Ma Tara's epiphany had seemingly left him.

Gopala urgently tried to gather himself. He closed his eyes, and willfully drove out of his mind all thoughts except those related to his beloved goddess. Like his guru, he sat perfectly still and waited. Slowly the trepidation subsided. He opened his eyes. "There is only One that is real," he replied. "There is only One existent entity."

Krishnadas reached down with his weather-beaten hand and placed it firmly around the stone icon. Gopala watched the teacher stroke it several times and then gradually raise the lingam to chest level. His heart fluttered.

The guru had observed his student closely enough over the past few months to recognize the substantial barriers he would have to overcome if he were to ever go beyond the state of just mouthing the truth and arrive at that ultimate condition of truly knowing it.

"Tell me, Gopala, what is this lingam then? What is this image of Shiva's power that both men and women worship?"

"It is only an illusion," the pupil responded with a small stutter. "It is merely a mirrored manifestation drawn from the web of maya."

"And tell me O student, what exactly is this web of maya and how do we account for its existence?" During his questioning Krishnadas moved his hand back and forth, all the while peering directly at the point on Gopala's forehead where he had earlier spread the sandal paste.

Gopala's ears started to tingle and his heart rate increased. He removed his eyes from the lingam and followed Krishnadas' lead by focusing them on the teacher's forehead. "It is the mistake of believing that the part is somehow separate from the whole. It is believing the drop to be distinct from the ocean. It is the mind's projection of its own ignorance."

Krishnadas returned the lingam to the ground. "And tell me O student, O one who takes such questions seriously, exactly what is that ocean of which you speak?"

"It is that which is existent, that which has being, that which truly is. It is that which the ancient sages called Brahman."

Krishnadas brought his hands together and slowly and methodically shook his head from side to side. "You must always remember, Gopala, that Brahman is neither existent nor non-existent. Brahman neither is, nor is not."

Gopala bit the inside of his bottom lip and looked down. Not only were his primary bodily energies engaged in a continual battle with his will, but now his mind was being confronted with the ultimate of paradoxes. He waited and then again shifted his eyes to meet those of his guru. "I do not understand," he mumbled.

Krishnadas could sense Gopala's growing despair and knew when it was appropriate to switch from questions to explanations.

"The meaning is this," he swiftly replied. "All words are limited when it comes to grasping the essence of Brahman. Words are like the various signs at railway stations. They indicate the name of the town or city, but they are not in themselves the town or city. Thus we must see that all language, even that of the most holy scriptures, is ultimately inadequate. Indeed, we can even go so far as to say that words themselves are the very foundation of illusory maya. Is this not affirmed in the Upanishadic texts themselves? Is this not the inherent meaning behind the Upanishadic claim that in reality there are as many universes as there are human beings? Every single person, no matter how insightful he might be, is bound to maya by the mere fact that he must of necessity make use of language, if not to speak it, then at least to think it. The closest we can get to the essence of reality through the use of words is via negation, neti neti; not this, not that."

Gopala thought carefully. "I do not mean to be disrespectful," he said, "for I am a mere student, but if what you have just said is true, then was not your earlier question, which was built upon words, illusory in nature?"

"I can see you are beginning to understand, Gopala," Krishnadas answered. "Yes, you are beginning to understand. Thought can never penetrate reality. This is because Brahman is like a shiny mirror. It is continually presenting us with a mere reflection of what we seek. Only immediate insight that breaks free from all objects, all words, all concepts, and all feelings will allow us to cross over the river of being and non-being."

Krishnadas' brief sermon on the impotence of words raised no further objections from his student. For as long as he could remember Gopala had intuitively believed this to be so. But he also sensed that the guru had not made his final point, and his supposition was quickly confirmed when Krishnadas again returned to his original topic.

"So, the correct answer to the question as to whether this lingam is real, is conditional in nature. If one is not attached to the lingam, then it is real. If one is attached to the lingam, then it is not real, for it is feeling, not thought, that determines both the nature of maya and the nature of the real."

Krishnadas again picked up the lingam, but this time he thrust it directly in front of Gopala's face. Gopala's mouth pulled back and his cheeks quivered. The guru could identify the clear and evident signs of a culminating inner tension, and he was prepared for what he knew from experience to be the first manifestations of a swift and onrushing delirium.

"Now, clear your mind," he thundered at Gopala while placing the lingam back on the ground. "Pierce through the womb of your mental attachment. Remember, behind all illusion lies the real, and reality is, in truth, the nothing that lies behind all nothingness."

The sharpness of Krishnadas' voice startled Gopala, and despite his increasing dizziness, he automatically followed the guru's instructions. He closed his eyes, focused his energies on the middle of his forehead, and began to meditate on the image of Ma Tara.

"Now, tell me exactly what it is that you see, Gopala," Krishnadas demanded after several minutes of intense observation. "Calmly and without passion describe to me exactly what you see," he repeated.

"I see Ma," Gopala replied, "nothing but Ma."

"Then your mind is not totally clear," Krishnadas shouted. "Clear your mind, Gopala. Go beyond Ma."

"That I cannot do," Gopala shouted in return. "It is hopeless. I cannot raise my mind above my beloved."

Krishnadas reached out and impulsively grasped Gopala's limp hand. He squeezed it with all of his might, and then thrust it down onto the lingam. "Go beyond Ma," he yelled. "Go beyond Ma."

Gopala tried desperately to pull away, but Krishnadas was much stronger than his student and held on tightly. "Go beyond Ma," the guru repeated yet again. "You must go beyond Ma."

Gopala's arms started to shake. Sweat covered his torso. For a second time he attempted to break free, yet try as he might he could not loosen his teacher's grasp. He closed his eyes tightly and cried out to Ma Tara. Now he could no longer see her; his mind was saturated with the image of the lingam. He began to choke. He knew that he was going to die. His stomach tensed; he waited.

What Krishnadas saw next both astonished and excited him. Gopala's hair stood out straight from his scalp, and his eyes rolled far back into his head. His hand vibrated with so much energy that the guru was forced to drop it, and when he did so, the young man toppled over on his side. Krishnadas continued to observed the prone young man. Gopala's condition remained the same. The guru had heard of such intense experiences associated with samadhi, but he had always thought that these stories were mainly the residue of wishful thinking and legend. Now he knew otherwise. In almost childish awe, he lay down next to his student.

Gopala remained in this transfixed state for more than six hours. When at last he had returned to normal consciousness, Krishnadas bent down and touched his forehead to his student's feet. "In one single blow, you have consumed Shiva's lingam and thereby cleaved Ma Tara in two," he said without looking up. "You have become a tirthankara, one who has crossed over."

The still dazed guru stood upright, balanced himself and disappeared from the hut.

Chapter 9

As many of you know, my Hindu brothers, even among the sons of India there are those who would have us surrender our great heritage to the Western imperialists. If they have not directly converted to Christianity, they have disguised their conversion with the name of Hindu reform. They speak out against our gods, they speak out against our time-honored traditions, and they would have India become not only a political colony of England, but a colony of the spirit as well. If the truth be told, my brothers, these men are no longer Hindus. They are little brown Englishmen."

The speaker paused. Thunderous cheers of approval rang out from his audience.

Jai Lal Rai stood only a little over five feet in height, but his booming voice and fiery expressions made him appear much larger. Like many of those listening to his stirring oration, Jai Lal was dressed in a traditional white cotton coat and pants. The paleness of his garments contrasted dramatically with his heavily oiled black hair and large brown eyes. The front of the hand-carved, wooden dais from which he spoke featured an intricately engraved black Om. The sacred symbol was encircled by an expansive, glistening, yellow sphere. Behind him a massive purple and gold swastika draped the wall.

"We must not be fooled. The very existence of our Hindu religion is currently being threatened. Let there be no doubt about this. If the so-called reformers are allowed to have their way now, future generations of Hindus will surely inherit little more than an Indian brand of Christianity. What began as a movement that told us how we should worship our gods, or at what age our sons and daughters should be allowed to be married, will inevitably end up as a crusade to banish our sacred texts and demolish our temples."

From the back of the hall, several young men started to chant: "Long live Hindu dharma; Victory to Mother India." Other men sitting near them followed their lead. Before long the entire room was engulfed in an ocean of pulsating sound.

Jai Lal Rai did not dampen the enthusiasm. He watched and waited. Eventually he raised his hands. "Brothers," he yelled at the top of his voice, but the crowd continued to chant. "Brothers," he cried out yet again. This time he energetically waved his arms from side to side. "Brothers, please give me your attention!"

The chorus slowly subsided. The room returned to its previous calm. Only the sound of periodic whispers interrupted the silence.

"We are indeed very fortunate," Jai Lal resumed, "to have here with us tonight one of the newest and, might I personally add, most prominent members of our fraternity, Manindra Gupta from Benares, who has kindly consented to address us."

Jai Lal moved aside and motioned in the direction of the front row. Manindra left his seat and, to the sound of thundering applause, arrived at the podium. He too was finally forced to try and bring the room to silence by frantically waving his hands above his head and raising his voice to the level of a shout.

The room turned hauntingly quiet.

"O sons of our beloved homeland," Manindra began, "let me start by saying that I feel it is terribly important to recognize we are living at a very crucial time in the history of our civilization. On the political front, we continue to be the victims of the Western imperialists who drain us economically and maintain their rule by the policy of divide and conquer. This in itself is a great crime that demands rectification, one for which the martyrs of 1857 stand as heroic witnesses. But at least for the moment, reality tells us we cannot expel the foreigner by force of arms. Like the Muslims before them, the British have taken advantage of the divisions among Hindus and gained a dominating political position. . . . So, the question arises, is the situation a hopeless one? Are we fated to remain impotent in all arenas of life?"

Before Manindra could answer his own questions, ripples of "no" and "never" spread across the room.

"You are right, my brothers. The answer is no! For what we do have is the foundation of our religion, which has survived over the millennia despite the continual onslaught of the numerous malignant forces that would attempt to destroy it. It is this religion that will provide us with the strength to eventually overcome our foreign rulers and once again become the masters of our own destiny."

Shouts of affirmation rang out once more from the assemblage, and Manindra had to again hold up his hands to regain the audience's attention. "But this is not all," he bellowed, "and here it is of utmost importance to realize the significance of what our dear brother Jai Lal Rai was saying."

Manindra leaned heavily on the podium and scanned the sea of spirited faces. "We must make very sure that we protect the foundations of our beloved civilization from those who would seek to undermine it. And here, my brothers, the greatest danger comes not from foreign politicians, nor even from Christian missionaries, but from within our own ranks . . . from those who brother Jai Lal has correctly called 'little brown Englishmen.' These people have not only been conquered politically, they have had their souls taken from them, and now they wish to take ours from us."

From different areas of the room sporadic shouts of "never" and "victory to Hindu dharma" permeated the air.

"Never indeed," Manindra replied, "but to prevent our religion from being destroyed from within we must do more than gather at meetings and identify the enemy. We must have some method, some plan of action."

Manindra allowed his observation to sink in.

"And what should that be?" yelled a man from the far back of the room.

Manindra had anticipated the query and launched into his prepared answer. "In my very humble opinion, sir, we must make use of our two most formidable resources: our manpower and our temples. Across this land we must find our best young men, those who are expertly trained in the knowledge of our religion and who in turn can train others as disciples to carry our message not only throughout India but into the very heartland of our enemy—England itself. We must not fight a solely defensive battle; we must also take the offensive. We must not become satisfied with merely begging for the existence of our spiritual heritage; we must prove its natural superiority. We should not just be asking for equality with Christianity. We must demonstrate that in the face of the knowledge of the Vedanta, Christianity is an inferior creed."

Another wave of applause extended across the room. Manindra calmly waited for it to subside.

"And this is where our temples become important," he went on. "They should be used as bases for recruiting and training our young men. These sacred spots, which are the spiritual hearts and nerve centers of our Hindu religion, must now become the focal points of a new Hindu renaissance . . . a renaissance that will not create puppets who bow down to our oppressors in the name of reform, but a renaissance that will send forth brave young men who, like heroes of bygone days, will stand unflinchingly before the demon and proudly assert their beliefs."

"Yes, yes," men hollered. "Long live Hindu dharma; Victory to Mother India."

Manindra did not bother to wave his hands aloft. "We are indeed fortunate," he shouted . . . "We are fortunate at the Ma Tara temple in Benares to have found such a young man. Although he is still in his twenties, he has become the living embodiment of our great Hindu teachings. He has recently taken the name Shri Jayananda. He possesses the heroic courage associated with the glorious name of Rama . . . His supreme meditative powers have taken him to that realm of blissful being we associate with the great saints of the past. He is currently educating a group of disciples who will hopefully carry his teachings and practices further afield, and with the support of an organization such as this one, I am sure we can be successful in our quest."

"We will support you," came a cry from the audience. "Victory to Shri Jayananda; Victory to Hindu dharma." Several other men joined in, and again there arose an avalanche of voices chanting affirmations.

"And one last thing, my dear brothers." Manindra was now pushing his voice to its limits. "It is my sincere hope that our successes will help create a network of teachers and acharyas who will build bridges with other temple complexes throughout our homeland, thereby bringing about a new Hindu unity that will allow us to accomplish the very goals we have been voicing here tonight. Remember, 'united we stand; divided we fall.'"

Manindra backed away from the podium. The audience abandoned any sense of restraint and began chanting in unison, "Victory to Shri Jayananda; Victory to Hindu dharma; Victory to Mother India!"

Chapter 10

The last of the disciples reverently bent down and softly placed his outstretched hands on the tirthankara's feet. He briefly mumbled a salutation, straightened his back and departed the room leaving the master alone in his meditative position. Jayananda remained motionless and reflected upon the recent chain of events that had so rapidly transformed him from a student into a teacher.

Not long after Krishnadas had declared him a "conqueror" and bestowed upon him the Jain epithet of tirthankara, Manindra started bringing Jayananda groups of young men with instructions from Harish to educate them in the knowledge of the Vedanta. Then one day Manindra informed him that the Ma Tara temple was part of a nation-wide effort to return Hinduism to its ancient glory, and that he could expect the number of new disciples under his tutelage to continue to grow. It was by no means an easy metamorphosis, and behind the apparent formality of the guru-disciple interchange, there still existed within Jayananda's mind a sense of inauthenticity. For one thing, he had found it extremely difficult to adopt a new name, and therefore it took some time before the sound of "Shri Jayananda" coming out of his students' mouths became acceptable to his psyche.

He had come to the realization that the teachings and ascetic practices of Krishnadas were more in tune with mature, adult spirituality, and he could now understand that many of his earlier 'episodes' had actually verged on the threshold of insanity. Still, honesty required him to also admit that deep within he was experiencing a certain sense of loss. Manindra often directly dictated the doctrines he currently taught to his disciples, and though he both knew and could articulate these teachings almost at will, they more-often-than-not left him uninspired. Were it not for his superlative meditative powers and his ability to reach samadhi so quickly and easily, he wondered if he would have attracted any followers at all.

All of these changes had also caused him to secretly resent Manindra, and he often longed for the days when Harish was more directly involved in running the affairs of the temple. Of course he understood that as the owner of the temple, Harish was a very busy man, and his position necessitated that he often travel outside of the city on business, but his sentiments in this regard could not be totally alleviated by the knowledge of practical considerations.

Normally at this time of day, Jayananda would first return to his household to look in on Chandramani and then go directly to meet with Manindra. On this occasion, however, he felt a sudden and urgent need to be alone. Thus, when he eventually terminated his meditation and exited the temple annex, he decided to take an alternative route, one that led him behind his house and in the direction of the compound's rear wall.

Jayananda passed through a deteriorating wooden archway and walked hurriedly in a northeasterly direction until he could see the gently rippling waters of the Ganges. He pressed forward, all the while carefully looking for a way down to the river. He located a pathway where the land sloped gradually to the bank. He reflexively followed its course and rapidly descended to the water's edge.

A short distance from the muddy bank, surrounded by the river's slowly moving currents, loomed a massive black rock whose oily-looking surface time had methodically worn smooth. Jayananda cautiously waded his way toward the diminutive island. He arrived at its base, placed his hands on the slick surface and carefully hoisted himself up. When he was completely out of the water, he folded his legs and automatically assumed the lotus position. He was not planning to meditate; he merely desired to sit still and silently observe the flow of life swirling busily around him. Thoughts of Lord Shiva seated atop his mighty Himalayan perch quietly looking down upon the world with a sense of detached serenity crossed the tirthankara's mind.

In the midst of this contemplation, Jayananda caught sight of a woman approaching the riverbank from the same hillock that he himself had traversed moments earlier. She was dressed in red robes and appeared to be carrying several books in her hands. Her hair was disheveled, and her gait was slow and rhythmical. Jayananda's first thought was that she must be a dancer or a prostitute, and he became filled with feelings of apprehension and repulsion. Still, he could not take his eyes off her, and when she reached the water and bent down to perform her ablutions, he found himself cautiously addressing her.

"What business have you here?" he asked.

The woman did not waver. She looked across at Jayananda. "I am in search of a certain tirthankara," she answered. "Last night I had a dream in which Ma Tara revealed to me that I would find him meditating near the Ganges."

Beneath the woman's ragged appearance, Jayananda could not help but notice her attractive facial features. Nevertheless, he remained concerned. "There are many such men," he stated.

"Indeed this is so," said the woman, "and that is why I must speak to him. I have been given certain signs."

Jayananda raised his eyebrows and flexed his shoulders. "And might I ask you just what these signs are?"

"There are four signs. First, he will be a devotee of Ma Tara and will have been initiated into the ranks of the shakta priesthood. Second, he will have agreed to marriage; not for himself, but for the sake of others. Third, he will carry within his heart the mark of Radha. And fourth, he will have temporarily abandoned his beloved."

Jayananda thought carefully about each of the four signs.

The first two were certainly clear enough, but he was somewhat confused about the third and fourth proofs. "This mark of Radha of which you speak, what is meant by it?" he asked.

The woman bent down and placed her bundle of books on the riverbank's dry, sandy surface. She seated herself in the identical posture as that of her questioner. She calmly closed her eyes, took several deep breaths through her nostrils, and then once again brought Jayananda's image into focus.

"The mark of Radha is a metaphor for one who has known the pain of separation from the beloved as intensely as Radha did when she was separated from Krishna," she declared. "A person who carries this mark has unashamedly cried out for their beloved in front of the world and has had their heart seared by the agony of the experience."

The female's words seeped into the inner recesses of Jayananda's mind. He slowly realized she was describing a part of himself. *The knowledge she possesses could only be the product of some innate, spiritual power*, he speculated. But he was not quite ready to place his trust in the woman.

"You say that this tirthankara has abandoned his beloved. But how can one who has reached the august station of tirthankara abandon his beloved?"

The woman smiled within. She knew from Jayananda's question that she had found the object of her search, but she feigned ignorance.

"A tirthankara is one who crosses over the river of existence and in so doing transcends the sorrows of life," she said. "The lover, on the other hand, accepts the pain of existence as the price he must pay for the experience of joy."

Jayananda instinctively retreated to the arguments he had learned while sitting at the feet of Krishnadas. "If a lover is attached to his beloved, then the beloved is not real," he concluded. "Only when the lover is not attached and goes beyond the snare of the emotions can the beloved be said to be real."

The woman sat and listened politely. Her face, however, spoke for her.

Jayananda read her expression. "You should study these matters."

"This teaching may appeal to your mind, O tirthankara, but your heart knows it not to be the only truth. You have allowed the doctrines of emotionally unsatisfied and resentful older men to submerge a segment of your soul. You have not completely crossed over the waters of illusion. You have been partially pushed beneath them."

Tingling sensations raced through Jayananda's limbs. He frantically attempted to take his psyche back to that day with Krishnadas when he had crossed over and became a tirthankara. He focused his thoughts on the guru's mental image and once again recalled his words: "Only immediate insight that breaks free from all objects, words, concepts, and feelings will allow us to cross over the river of being and non-being."

All of his willed effort was useless. He could feel his heart starting to give way. Successive images of Ram Das, his uncle, Harish, and finally Ma Tara flashed vividly through his mind. He tried to let go, but this time the images did not disappear. Meanwhile the woman had opened one of her books and began to sing in a melodious voice:

"O Radha, look at the dancers in the forest.
In springtime, there are numerous half-opened
    blossoms.
They await the pollen gatherer.
The sound of Krishna's flute has called.
Listen, . . . why do you drowse away?
Why do you delay?
O lady, the time goes vainly by.
The storm clouds gather.
The peacocks cry.
The birds and deer rejoice.
The river ceases flowing.
And still you do not act.
How long will it take you
To fly to your beloved?
O Radha, look at the dancers in the forest."

Jayananda lowered himself into the cool water and began to wade back across the river.

The woman seemed unperturbed by his approach. She maintained her pose and continued to sing her verses.

The tirthankara reached the bank and dropped to the sand. He touched the woman's feet. "I have much to learn from you," he said.

"And I have much to learn from you, O tirthankara," the woman replied.

Chapter 11

Jayananda sat on his haunches and patiently awaited the arrival of Rukhmini. The once brilliant sun was now well beyond its zenith. The shadows cast by several nearby tulsi trees continued to lengthen. Most of the tirthankara's disciples were busily engaged in performing their priestly tasks in one of the compound's numerous temples.

It had been six months since that day at the river when Jayananda first met Rukhmini. Then he did not know of her religious affiliation, and in his intuitive response to her words and verses, he had not even taken the question into consideration. Later he discovered she was in fact a bhairavi, a practitioner of the tantric rites, those 'left-handed' rituals that on the surface seemed to desecrate many of the traditional Hindu rites and customs with which he had been raised. This had caused him to reflexively shy away from her as if he had unexpectedly encountered an untouchable woman at the village well.

His withdrawal did not discourage Rukhmini. She proceeded to seek him out, declaring that Ma Tara had sent her to him to become his disciple. Over time, her dogged persistence impressed him, and he allowed her an audience. Moreover, there was something manifest within Rukhmini's personality that attracted Jayananda, and regardless of his own inner protests, as well as the frequent whisperings of several of his most prominent disciples, he soon found himself inviting her back to the temple compound.

After her next few visits Jayananda could not decide if Rukhmini was a saint or a demon. He turned to Ma Tara for an answer to his dilemma. Several nights of intense prayer and meditation resulted in the goddess speaking to him in a blazing vision. She revealed that the woman could do him no harm. Thereafter, Rukhmini was allowed to make regular sojourns to the temple.

Their meetings took place in a small grove located within shouting distance from the meditation hut in which Krishnadas had taught Jayananda the essence of the Vedanta. On these occasions, Rukhmini would offer several prayers to Ma Tara and read aloud a passage or two from one of her books. She would next turn to Jayananda and ask him to expound on the meaning of the verses. After he had spoken, she would offer her own comments based on the tantric teachings. Subsequently they would discuss the intricacies of their positions, sometimes for hours on end.

The relationship he established with the bhairavi was quite different from those Jayananda had forged with his male disciples. The young men nearly always lingered on every word that their master spoke and were anxious that they might disappoint him. Rukhmini was more playful. Sometimes she would even go so far as to admonish the tirthankara for what she felt were transparent interpretations.

At first Jayananda was taken aback by such boldness on her part, yet as time went on he progressively realized that the words he had proclaimed that first day at the river were true; he had much to learn from the bhairavi. In fact, the tirthankara had slowly begun to see Rukhmini as the feminine side of himself, an imagined Radha that danced with his inner Krishna. Now the sight of the woman coming towards him would instantly engender in his mind the image of Brindavan queen preparing herself to join her divine lover in the great circle dance of ras lila. All of his senses would become more acute and he would quickly forget whatever concerns cluttered his mind.

Rukhmini made her sudden appearance at the far end of the grove. Slowly she sauntered her way in the direction of the seated Jayananda. The tirthankara whispered beneath his breath sacred verses that he had known by heart since childhood: "To those in need, every grace proceeds from the princess Radha. Even Lord Krishna will seek without ceasing her merciful, mischievous, sidelong glance."

The bhairavi was within several feet of her guru before she brought her advance to a halt. She raised her hands together to a spot just in front of her mouth, bowed her head ever-so-slightly, and lowered her body to the ground. Gently she touched Jayananda's feet with her outstretched fingers.

"I see you have not brought any of your books today." Jayananda's tone lacked inflection.

The woman pushed herself up from the ground and sat down on the matted grass across from the tirthankara.

"Have you forgotten already, Shri Jayanandaji? At the conclusion of our last meeting you asked if the teachings I have been describing were not mere words from books. So today I decided not to bring my books."

Jayananda showed no visible signs of reaction. Inwardly he could only admire the woman for her tenacity.

"Well, then," he reacted after some time, "I can see that you understand the challenge. Today there will be no books, and there will also be no guru. Together we will find the essence of the tantra right here. For if these teachings contain certain truths, then these truths should be manifest in this grove at this very moment without teacher nor text."

Ma Tara is obviously guiding him, Rukhmini reasoned.

The bhairavi's thoughts did not linger. She reached down inside her robe and pulled out several large radishes which she had brought for her afternoon meal. She was aware that Jayananda was watching and took care to place the radishes equidistant from one another on the ground in front of her.

"O Shri Jayanandaji," she loudly proclaimed, "the essence of tantra is indeed visible in this grove at this very moment, for in truth these radishes are as sacred as that magnificent tulsi." Her finger pointed to a tree on the opposite side of the grove.

"Or this dirt . . ." She paused and lowered her hand to the ground to grasp several clumps of brown earth between her fingers. "These meager clods are as sacred as the Ganges that flows just over that ridge." Again she used her free finger to signify the object of her intent.

"I am in everything; Everything is in me."

"Yes," Rukhmini said instantaneously. "I am That."

Jayananda nodded his head in agreement.

"And in you, Shri Jayanandaji, I have seen the truth of these sanctified words expressed on numerous occasions with great power and utmost eloquence, but it is also true that there is a greater truth to be found in action than in words or ideas."

Before Jayananda could respond Rukhmini took the dirt that was still fresh in her hand, thrust it into her open mouth, and began to consume it.

The shocking sight of the woman eating the clods of dirt brought back to Jayananda memories of those days immediately following his uncle's death when he himself had periodically performed such bizarre stunts. Now, he cringed at the very thought.

"Whatever are you doing?" he cried.

"You were the one, Shri Jayananda, who asked for immediate manifestations of the tantric path and not mere words."

"But eating such things is impure. Only those of unsound mind perform such acts. Surely this cannot be a manifestation of truth."

Rukhmini chose her words deliberately. "Shri Jayanandaji. For some months now we have been discussing the sacred teachings relative to the principle of divine unity, and we have agreed that such a vision is indisputably at the core of both the Vedas and the Puranas. And this outlook is also the essence of the tantric path. In this regard, all three paths expound the belief that in the first state there is form, in the second state there is formlessness, and finally there is the state beyond form and formlessness."

"This is so."

"But the path of tantra is not satisfied with mere words. As you intuitively understood by asking me to show you the manifest truth of tantra existent in this grove here and now, spiritual truth is not just an abstract idea but a path of action. In tantra, we are taught that while many in established society may speak of divine unity, they have in actuality surrounded themselves with behaviors that fortify in their psyches the exact opposite of what they illustrate with their words. So it is, that one who is a follower of the tantric path is first taught to call good what others label as 'don't do this' or 'this shouldn't be done.' In eating this dirt I am directly demonstrating the truth of the principle of divine unity."

Jayananda intellectually understood what Rukhmini was saying, and could find no solid theological objection to her statements, but he still experienced a feeling of unease whose source he could neither identify nor exactly explain. Rukhmini sensed the tirthankara's ambivalence and again reached down to the ground and again filled her fingers with dirt. But this time instead of taking her hand to her own mouth, she extended it towards Jayananda.

Instinctively the tirthankara pulled his head away.

"Shame, disgust, and fear; these three shall not remain," Rukhmini said. "And there is only one way to banish these demons."

Jayananda knew precisely to what Rukhmini was referring, but he remained quiet. His piercing gaze told her, however, what she needed to know.

"Shri Jayanandaji, you must believe me when I say that Ma Tara herself has sent me to you to deliver this message. I know in truth that I am a mere nothing. I am not even worthy to be the dirt beneath your holy lotus feet. Ask the goddess if you must. She will speak to you. She wants you to receive the initiation, to become a master of all three sadhanas: Vedantic, puranic, and tantric."

The creases on Jayananda's forehead flattened. "It is time for me to go now," he said. "I am already late for my afternoon puja."

Rukhmini remained seated on the ground.

"Namaskar," he said.

Rukhmini returned the salutation.

Jayananda had turned in the direction of the temple when an unexpected afterthought seized him. There was a gleam in his eye. He stooped down, picked up two of the radishes and, with a smile on his face, dropped them into his mouth.

Chapter 12

It was a little past midnight. At last Jayananda was able to slip unnoticed out of his house. Since they did not share a common bedroom, he was fairly certain his movement had not disturbed Chandramani's slumber.

He passed unobtrusively through the garden and onto the adjacent foot path. The darkness provided by the new moon gave him the added assurance that even should he somehow be seen from a distance by a fellow priest or one of his own disciples, he would not be easily recognized.

Jayananda's destination was the local cremation grounds. He walked quickly and quietly. He knew the route well, and several times during his short trek he found himself thinking how he had visited the same cremation grounds almost daily for the first two weeks following Raychand's death. He also remembered with some vividness the occasions on which he had approached the edge of madness there, and this recollection brought with it a powerful flushing sensation. The reaction caused him to briefly contemplate abandoning his journey and returning to the temple grounds, but he willfully pushed such thoughts out of his mind and marched forward.

The tirthankara could tell from the barren features of the land around him that he was approaching his goal. Soon he could smell the scent of burned wood from the still-smoldering ashes of the day's final funeral pyres.

Earlier that morning Jayananda had arranged to meet with Rukhmini near the entryway to the grounds, and he was now close enough to start scanning the area for any sign of human form. The lack of moonlight made it rather difficult for him to see clearly, but it was not too long before Jayananda spotted the blurry outline of a shadowy figure standing motionless in the distance. He automatically steered his course in the apparition's direction.

Out of the darkness he was met with a sudden and forceful greeting. "Namaskar, Shri Jayanandaji."

The bhairavi was dressed for the occasion in a fresh red robe which was loosely draped both around her body and over the top of her head. Through the folds, a matching red underblouse periodically made an appearance. In one hand she held a tattered brown book. On the ground next to her feet there rested a sizable burlap bag. Her forehead was smeared with a mixture of vermilion paste and white ash. Each of her nostril's displayed two dainty gold rings.

Although she was not beautiful, the shape and carriage of her mouth, combined with her deep inset eyes, gave Rukhmini a mysteriously sensual look which, had he been so inclined, would have presented Jayananda's will with a formidable challenge.

"Namaskar, Mother," Jayananda replied in return.

Rukhmini stooped down and plucked up the bag. She gestured forward with her head and started walking. Jayananda followed close on her heels. The bhairavi had only traveled a short distance when the sound of her companion's frightened voice over her shoulder forced the woman to slow her pace.

"Don't go any further; I can see someone coming this way," Jayananda stated in a loud whisper.

"Yes, there are many others here this evening," she responded. "On those nights when the rituals are performed, a large number of people come to the cremation grounds."

"But I cannot afford to be seen," Jayananda pleaded in a slightly louder voice "If Harish were to find out . . . "

Rukhmini took a few more steps and then stopped. She turned back towards Jayananda, deliberately set the bag down at the side of her feet, and gently put her left hand upon the tirthankara's bare shoulder. "Do not worry Shri Jayananda," she said. "The tantric rituals are always performed in pairs, and each pair consummates the ritual alone. I can assure you that tonight you will only be with me . . . Believe me, there are a great many people here tonight who, like yourself, desire that the secrecy of their identity be maintained."

Rukhmini picked up the bag. "It is not much further," she said.

Jayananda trailed close behind the woman. All the while he kept hoping that the darkness would cover his identity from any passersby.

At an area where the dusty earth of the cremation grounds met with the murky waters of the Ganges, Rukhmini halted. She methodically searched around her and soon located what she was looking for: a patch of dry grass nestled up against several robust bushes. She swiftly advanced to the chosen spot, set her bag down on the ground, and gazed in the direction of the shadowy-rimmed new moon. "This location is an auspicious one," she authoritatively announced.

Jayananda followed Rukhmini to the selected site and sat down on the grass across from the bhairavi. He carefully scrutinized her movements. Systematically she removed several items from the bag and placed them on the ground next to her left knee.

Jayananda knew that tonight he would ritually partake of the five forbidden substances, objects that under normal conditions no clean Hindu would ever dare consume. In so doing he would demonstrate that there was nothing beyond the bounds of Ma Tara, that she was, in truth, manifest in all things, even those items considered by the pious to be impure. In the words that Rukhmini had taught him, "it was man and man alone who so divided the world into such categories; man and man alone who could speak of the oneness of all reality and then hypocritically proceed to divide the world of action into the 'thou shalls' and 'thou shall nots.'"

Rukhmini was ready to commence with the first portion of the rite. She whispered several long invocations to Ma Tara,

Shiva, and Vishnu and then reached back into the bag and brought out a bowl-like object, which, upon closer inspection, Jayananda realized was actually part of a human skull. Once this reality hit him, the tirthankara instantaneously recoiled in horror by violently pulling his head and arms to one side.

The bhairavi had anticipated such an intense reaction. Immediately, but calmly, she responded: "You must remember, Shri Jayananda, that the Lord Shiva and Ma Tara are the masters of both life and death. They know what we forget; namely, that in reality there is no essential difference between this skull and a baby's rattle. Is it not we ourselves who make such distinctions? Would you fear a baby's rattle?"

Jayananda returned his hands to his lap and inwardly called upon Ma Tara to aid him. Over and over, he silently repeated her name. Meanwhile Rukhmini removed from the bag several more items, including a small piece of uncooked flesh and a bottle of darkened liquid. Once more she whispered invocations to various deities. At the same time she placed the flesh into the skull and resolutely poured the dusky liquid over it. Then she raised the skull to her forehead. "This is thine essence, O Ma," she said three times.

The magical melody of Rukhmini's words caused Jayananda to experience a sudden surge of heat at the base of his spine. He repeated the bhairavi's phrase: "This is thine essence, O Ma," he affirmed. "This is thine essence."

The final words were barely out of Jayananda's mouth when Rukhmini was again vigorously chanting: "Speak to me, O speaker of Speech," she cried. "Establish thyself firmly on the tip of my tongue, O thou who bringest all truth under control."

The bhairavi lowed the skull to the level of her heart and touched it three times to her breast. "O thou primordial power that is coiled like a snake at both the center of our individual beings and the center of the entire universe, I meditate upon thee and envision thee rising gloriously above my head and pouring into thy disciple's mouth this sacred substance as an offering to thine own truth."

Rukhmini arose and pointed the skull it in the direction

of the darkened moon. She touched it to Jayananda's head and heart and again invoked Ma Tara. "O Primal Mother, O Eternal Partner of Lord Shiva," she said, "only Thou does truly exist."

The skull was now directly in front of Jayananda's face. Slowly he opened his mouth and allowed Rukhmini to pour between his lips the skull's consecrated contents. Even though a strong, spicy sauce disguised the meat, when his taste buds first experienced the pungent flesh, they revolted, and a gagging sensation threatened to overcome him. He did not panic, however, but simply closed his eyes and used all of his will to maintain control. Gradually, the feeling subsided.

The same ritual was repeated another three times. On each occasion, the bhairavi placed a new substance into the skull: a piece of salty fish, followed by several grains of parched barley, and finally, a mouthful of bitter rice wine. Except for the charred barley, the tirthankara's response to each new ingredient was virtually the same: a violent choking sensation that required a tremendous personal effort to control.

Rukhmini was ready for the final act of the tantric drama. For the last time she consecrated the skull with a litany of invocations before gently placing it back in the bag. She sat upright and softly called upon Ma Tara to bless her mind, body, and soul. For a short while she remained perfectly still, and then with a few hurried movements of her hands she intertwined her fingers, leaned backwards, and directed her palms upward. "It is time to taste of the divine lotus," she pronounced. Almost concurrently she began repeating the very same verses that had accompanied the earlier stages of the ritual.

Rukhmini concluded her recitation. Jayananda leaned forward. As he did so, his arms started to tremble uncontrollably. This was the portion of the initiation which he had feared the most. He continued to shake. He fervently called upon Ma Tara for help: "You have given your permission, Ma," he whispered in a quivering voice. "Do not abandon me now."

"Come taste of the thousand-petaled lotus of eternity, Shri Jayananda," Rukhmini called out in an effort to encourage the tirthankara. "Make of this sacred blossom a divine offering to all the gods." The coolness of the evening air could not prevent a thin layer of moisture from gathering on Jayananda's shoulders and forehead. He closed his eyes, and in the manner of the four previous substances called upon his inner volition. Instead of gaining control, this time he merely began to feel dizzy. He experienced a sudden dropping sensation and—

Rukhmini watched Jayananda lurch back onto his haunches. His hair stood out straight, and his eyes rolled upward. Small sparks intermittently jumped from the skin on his neck and upper arms. The bhairavi had seen the tirthankara go into deep samadhi on numerous occasions, but never so suddenly or dramatically. She sat up and stared at him in absolute wonderment.

"Not the lotus, but the goat's head," the tirthankara blurted out in a voice that Rukhmini had never before heard from him. "Not the lotus, but the goat's head." This phrase was repeated several more times before Jayananda drooped to one side, briefly looked up and then collapsed on the dirt.

Jayananda had regained consciousness. Rukhmini helped him to his feet, and together they made their way out of the cremation grounds.

"Forgive me," Jayananda kept saying. "I do not know what came over me."

"For some reason Ma Tara did not feel that the occasion was appropriate," the bhairavi responded "It will happen in time. There will be other initiations. All is in her hands." Then she bowed and disappeared into the darkness.

Jayananda's short walk to the top of the hill was shrouded in confusion. *Was it my arrogant pride*, he kept asking himself, *or was it rather a warning from Ma Tara? But how could that be? She gave me her permission.*

He reached the end of his climb. His thoughts were interrupted by sounds coming from a short distance down the nearby road. He listened closely and promptly recognized them as the slowly dissipating clatter of horses' hoofs. He squinted and made out the image of a small black carriage whose back was lined with two large brass plates. He could have sworn it was Harish's.

Chapter 13

Harish was dying. The temple owner had known for some time that he was not well, but he had largely ignored his illness. Even when he finally forced himself to consult a Western physician, and learned that his body was diagnosed with stomach cancer, he was able to keep the seriousness of his condition a secret from both his family and friends by passing it off as a combination of anemia and overwork. But as the cancer grew, and the noticeable changes in his skin color and energy levels became ever more manifest, Harish was eventually forced to confide in those closest to him that he did not have much time to live and that when he passed Manindra would take charge of temple affairs. Inevitably, the day came when he could no longer get out of his bed, and soon thereafter a constant stream of visitors began arriving to say their final farewells.

When Jayananda first heard about Harish's terminal condition, he did not leave the confines of his house for three consecutive days. Though passionate in their content, his numerous prayers to Ma Tara seemed to go unheeded, and his temporary loss of intimacy with the goddess led to ever-increasing bouts of melancholy. The feelings that now invaded his conscious hours were those that had haunted him following the deaths of both his father and uncle. This rekindled sense of morbidity caused him to call into question his own spiritual powers. He could worship the goddess in a variety of forms, flawlessly teach the many doctrines of both bhakti and

Vedantic Hinduism, and almost at will make himself fall into a state of mystical rapture, yet the nagging worm had reemerged in his soul. He understood it to mean that while he was commonly called a tirthankara, he had not really passed beyond the river of existence. At times he sensed, if only subconsciously, that he did not even desire to go beyond the wheel of life.

His emotional reaction to Harish's approaching death had shown Jayananda that he could not detach himself from this man by simply saying, "all things must pass," or "the world is a passing fantasy." The world of form, the world of the here and now, the joys of maya, were still very much with him. And if the truth be told, was not this attraction to the 'grand play' one of the reasons he had been so fascinated by Rukhmini's teachings?

Even after the initial impact of the news of Harish's state had lost its sharper edges, Jayananda could still not bring himself to go to the house and see his benefactor. It was as if something deep within his psyche was attempting to play the old childhood trick whereby a refusal to admit the truth would somehow make that truth magically disappear.

As time went on, and Harish's condition continued to deteriorate, Jayananda came to accept the fact that he would have to force himself to gather up the required courage to go to the man's bedside. Not only did he desire to see and touch the flesh of the live Harish one last time, he also felt the continuing need to unburden himself of his own spiritual dilemma. He had recently concluded that he was no longer capable of representing the temple, and with this realization came the increased awareness that it was his moral duty to reveal the truth to the owner before he departed the world.

The morning on which Jayananda eventually made his decision to go visit Harish was a glorious one. Warm and gusty overnight winds from out of the northwest had cleared away the thin layer of smoky haze that often hung over the city and caused it to look like a spruced up village the day after the annual spring cleaning. Both natural and man-made objects appeared larger and more radiant than usual. The air was infused with a sweet scent of purity.

Jayananda made his way across the compound and approached Harish's house. His spirits were beginning to lift. The thought of death was still with him, but the surrounding beauty of the morning and the penetrating freshness of the air had once again reminded him of the perpetual power of rebirth. The dancing Shiva with his sword of destruction was beginning to give way to the youthful Krishna and his playful flute.

The tirthankara was met at the door by one of the numerous servants that now filled the household. The man took the visitor into the parlor where, following a wait of several minutes, he met briefly with Kamala. He assured Harish's wife that the stay would be a short one, whereupon the woman ordered another servant to take him to Harish's room. He found the owner lying quietly on his bed. Two thick quilts covered the lower part of his body, and several full-bodied silk pillows propped up his back and head.

Jayananda walked gingerly up to the bed. He immediately noticed the sallowness of Harish's gaunt face and the heaviness of his half-closed eyelids. Unaccountably he dropped to his knees and put his hands on the man's blanket-covered feet.

"No, no, Jayananda," Harish rasped. "I am not the tirthankara. Get up. I want to see your charming face."

Jayananda obeyed and sluggishly stood up. His shoulders drooped, his eyes became watery and his hands started to twitch. "And I also am not the tirthankara, Harish Babu," he whispered.

"Do not speak such nonsense," replied Harish in a tone of voice which indicated that Jayananda's words had suddenly energized him. The owner's eyes were now wide open and his body leaned in the direction of his visitor. "It is common knowledge that Ma Tara speaks through you," he continued. "And there is no question whatsoever that you are the bearer of special powers."

Jayananda lowered his head. "But I am still too attached to the world," he said. "I have not been able to cross over."

Harish reached out and gently took hold of Jayananda's hand. "Your main problem, my dear Jayananda, is that you have been striving too hard to climb up to the Absolute, as if the Absolute could only be experienced above and away from this world. And perhaps this is somewhat my fault, in that I may have bowed too hastily to Manindra's desire that the temple should emphasize the Vedantic path, but you must remember that the Absolute can also be experienced in the world. Many of our great saints have known this truth. They have taught it as the doctrine of divine immanence, and it is this intuitive knowledge that I have always seen present in you."

Jayananda listened carefully to the owner's message. He gradually tightened his hold on the dying man.

"What you and I both inherently know," Harish went on, "is that when we worship the image of Ma Tara, we are in reality revering the great goddess in the form of her universal manifestation. But what is more, my beloved Jayananda, when I notice the unreserved devotion with which you worship Ma Tara in the sanctuary of her own temple, when I observe the sanctified rapture that overcomes you during those glorious moments when you communicate with the divine form of the goddess, I see that you understand this sacred truth in a very special way that others do not."

Jayananda could feel the pressure of Harish's hand pushing upwards and let go of his fingers. The owner reached up and lightly touched the young man's face. "In a very special way," he repeated.

"But, Harish Babu, it is not only the stone image of Ma Tara to which I am attached, I am also attached to . . ." Jayananda could not bring himself to complete the sentence.

Harish did not hesitate with his answer. "Believe me, I know . . . Think of it this way; if one can worship the goddess in a stone image, then why can she not be adored in her living embodiments?"

"Manindra Babu would never accept such an approach." Jayananda murmured. "He would undoubtedly see it as a lack of spiritual strength, or perhaps even worse."

Harish smiled. "Let us just say that Manindra has a taste for the ascetic," he answered, "or at least in theory." The smile broadened. "But in any case, you should not be overly concerned with what Manindra thinks. Moreover, you can supply him with what he needs and still worship Ma Tara."

Jayananda weakly shook his head and squinted. "I do not understand what you mean, Harish Babu. Can you please explain?"

Harish slowly shifted his body so that the majority of his weight was now centered on his right side. "Listen closely," he said. "It is not required within the temple community that all beliefs or modes of worship be the same for all people. I have managed the temple for many years, and I learned this truth very early on. You must have noticed that there are those in the community who are not capable of understanding certain truths. And this is quite normal. In fact, the community can be divided roughly into three groups: the providers, or those who support the temple with their financial resources and regular devotion; the 'outer circle,' those priests, temple attendants and disciples who are able to follow the outer forms of religion; and the 'inner circle,' those who can penetrate through the mere forms of religion to the deeper spiritual truths that it harbors. And, as you know and have experienced, these more profound truths are often paradoxical in nature . . .

Now, it is certainly true that you must be able to provide leadership for all of these groups, but in so doing, you do not have to require of a provider what you demand of a member of the outer circle, nor give to a member of the outer circle what you share with those in the inner circle. Do you understand?"

Jayananda hesitated. "So you are saying, Harish Babu, that Manindra is a member of the outer circle?"

"Precisely."

For some time both men remained quiet. Jayananda contemplated Harish's advice. The temple owner wondered if that advice had been sufficiently understood.

"Do not misunderstand me." Harish said at last. "Manindra is a very spiritual man, but he has eyes and ears for only certain truths, and while these are very powerful truths, they are not the only truths . . . Manindra wants the temple to represent what he understands to be the martial teachings of our Hindu tradition, and these teachings are unquestionably there to be found. You can give those to him, but you can also teach the secret truths."

The word 'secret' resonated throughout Jayananda's consciousness and brought to the forefront of his mind his meetings with Rukhmini and his connection with the tantras. He understood what he had to do next. The trembling returned to his hands.

"Harish Babu." The words were little more than whispers. "There is something else that I need to tell you."

Harish knew what Jayananda was about to say to him, but he responded otherwise. "And what is that?"

Jayananda managed the strength to look directly into Harish's expiring eyes. "For some time now I have been keeping the company of . . . of some followers of the tantric path. The truth is, that I have found myself becoming attracted to many of their teachings, and Ma Tara . . ."

Harish slowly and difficultly raised his left hand up from the bed and briefly gestured with his curled forefingers for Jayananda to stop. "Yes, I know all about your investigation and study of the tantric teachings," he acknowledged. "Rukhmini has told me what a marvelous student you are."

The young man could hardly believe what he had just heard. "Then you know about this?" was all he could think to say.

"Oh, my dear one." Harish again took hold of Jayananda's hand and gave it a soft squeeze. "The truth is not for everyone's ears. Does not even the goddess herself keep secrets from her Shiva? Some doors are opened; some doors are closed . . . and some doors are meant to remain a secret."

Harish's last sentence jolted Jayananda. The owner recognized the affect his words were having on him and slowly repeated them three more times.

The mantra-like sound of Harish's voice instilled fresh energy into the tirthankara. What had moments before seemed contradictory now appeared to fall into place. In some mysterious way Harish's words had pierced into the heart of his psyche and put to flight the opposing forces that had been waging battle in his soul.

"Of course," he whispered, "Of course." He dropped to his knees, and against the man's protestations began fervently praising Harish's name to the goddess.

One of the servants appeared unannounced in the doorway. "Mama says it is time for your afternoon nap," he proclaimed.

Jayananda quickly stood up.

Harish unhesitatingly waved the man away with his left hand. "Tell mama that I will only be a few more minutes," he answered.

The servant did not leave.

Jayananda looked across at the man and then back at Harish.

The owner saw the question in the tirthankara's eyes. "A few more moments are not going to do me any harm," he repeated. "Anyway, I will quite soon enough be able to sleep completely undisturbed." Again he signaled to the man to leave.

Even after this second attempt to get him to depart the servant stubbornly stood his ground. "Mama says right now."

"You should do as Mama wishes," Jayananda said. "As you wisely taught me, wives must be answered to." For the first time since he had entered the room, Jayananda had a smile on his face.

"Yes, it is true that a wife cannot be ignored," Harish agreed, "but there are times when a man must have the final say." He struggled to look back at the servant. "Did you not hear me? I said just another few minutes." This time his voice was more demanding. "Remember, I can still have you dismissed."

The servant finally took heed and retreated.

"Now, one last thing, my dear Jayananda . . . Rukhmini told me about the evening at the cremation ground and what you said while you were in samadhi."

Jayananda shrugged his shoulders and turned his hands inward. "I am not aware of what I said. Rukhmini has never mentioned anything to me about this."

"Well, she spoke to me, and your words were: 'Not the lotus but the goat's head.'" Harish's voice dropped to a virtual whisper.

Jayananda still looked perplexed.

"And what is more," continued Harish, "she also explained the hidden meaning behind your utterance."

Kamala appeared in the doorway. Harish saw her and hurriedly gestured to Jayananda to come close. The young man bent down and put his ear next to Harish's mouth.

"It is time for you to leave, Shri Jayananda," Kamala declared as her husband quickly whispered something to his visitor. "Harish Babu must get his rest. You are welcome to come again tomorrow afternoon if you wish."

Jayananda left the room with his thoughts clinging to the words that Harish had breathed into his ear. That night as the tirthankara lay in his room and contemplated his future with a sense of renewed vigor, Harish quietly passed away in his sleep.

Chapter 14

And tell me, Govinda, how do you think you fared on your recent exams?"

The questioner was Bhabanath Narayan, a young man in his early twenties who was busy pushing back the side strands of his jet-black hair with the oily palms of his cupped hands. Periodically he admired his own good looks by peering into the fractured glass of a small wall-mirror.

"All in all, dear cousin, I believe that my performance was a good one." Govinda Narayan was also blessed with striking good looks and thick, rich, black hair, but whereas Bhabanath was often preoccupied with things physical, Govinda was generally more modest about his appearance.

"Actually, I had anticipated the question they asked about Hume's epistemology, so I am fairly sure that I did relatively well on that one, but the question on Locke was not quite what I had expected. Still, all in all, I think I should get my first levels."

In contrast to Govinda, Bhabanath had never been an outstanding student. From an early age he had longed to push aside the world of abstract ideas and become involved in the action of everyday life. As soon as he had finished fifth form, he left school to join his father's clothing business. Still, he did not like to let on that he lacked an academic background, so although he did not understand the meaning of the bookish-sounding word that his cousin had just used, he did not bother to ask Govinda what it meant but nonchalantly extended the conversation. "And then what? Is it on to law school?" he asked.

"Well, that is certainly what father wants."

"But what do you want?"

"To to be honest with you, Bhabanath, I am not sure what I really want. Eventually, I would like to continue my studies. For now, I think I need a break."

"Whatever would you propose to do Govinda?" Bhabanath took one last long look in the mirror. "All you know, my dear little cousin, is books and ideas."

Govinda deposited his books on a nearby table and fell into a large cushioned chair. "Several things have crossed my mind. For one thing, I thought that I might travel for a while, perhaps visit some other cities and towns. We have relatives all over northern India. I could certainly stay with them."

"But why would you want to do that?"

Govinda was uncertain how to answer. "All of my knowledge is book knowledge," he said in an exasperated burst. "Unlike you, I know hardly anything about how the world works or what the real India is like."

"And what is this real India of which you speak, Govinda?" Bhabanath was now standing above him.

Again Govinda searched for the right words. "You know what I mean . . . I am referring to such things as customs, beliefs, religious and caste practices, and how people from different walks of life really live. I can recite English political philosophy almost without error, but when it comes to these matters, outside of the family rituals I am almost totally ignorant, even of our own religion."

"Well, if what you want is to learn about religion, then you do not have to leave this city of ours to fulfill your desire. There is certainly no lack of gurus or acharyas here who can teach you just about anything you want to know. This very evening I have been invited by Hriday to go and see his guru from the Ma Tara temple. From what I hear, he has become quite the rage, even beyond Benares. If you would like to join us, I am sure Hriday would not care."

Govinda thought about the offer. "And what makes this guru so special?"

"To tell you the truth, Hriday has been rather guarded in what he has told me about his teacher. As I recall, his name is Shri Jayananda, and from what I can understand, he is part of a national movement that has dedicated itself to the revival of the ancient glories of Hinduism. But Hriday did mention that he can be rather unconventional at times."

Bhabanath's comment piqued Govinda's interest. "And whatever is that supposed to mean?" he inquired.

"Apparently Shri Jayananda has been known to go into deep samadhi and subsequently do some pretty bizarre things."

"Like what?"

"Well, for one, act like he is one of Krishna's gopis, or . . ." Bhabanath laughed, "pretend he is Sita."

"Rama's Sita?"

Bhabanath nodded his head. "That is what Hriday told me," he confirmed, "but he also warned that such revelations are generally only for his close disciples, so I doubt that we would encounter such a performance tonight. Still, one never knows, and it sounds as if it could be an interesting evening."

"I certainly have nothing better to do," said Govinda.

Bhabanath looked pleased. "Very well," he said. "The Ma Tara temple is well within walking distance from here, and Hriday said that he would meet me there just before sundown. I can drop by and pick you up if you wish."

"I will be waiting."

"Good . . . and now I have some errands to run."

"And I have to take a nap."

Bhabanath let out a deep laugh and firmly flicked Govinda on the top of the head with his outstretched forefinger. On his way to the door he made one last stop at the mirror, again pushed back the sides of his hair and made his exit.

To loud and intermittent shouts of "long live Shri Jayananda," and "victory to the guru," the tirthankara entered the room that was the annex to the Ma Tara temple and seated himself upon a purple and pale blue silk-lined cushion. The smell of recently lit incense slowly wafted through the air. At the back of the room stragglers scurried to find places to sit.

More than fifteen years had passed since Harish's death. During this time Jayananda had increasingly come to better understand both the disparate levels of complexity within the temple community as well as the varied requirements of his role as its spiritual leader, but he still did not feel comfortable with the more visible dimension of his vocation. He much preferred being alone with his hand-picked disciples, that inner circle of dynamic young men with whom he could share his deepest spiritual insights, than being on stage mouthing religious platitudes to hundreds of nameless souls, some devout, but some also just curious. Nevertheless, he knew that Manindra's public needs required mollification, and hence he had consented to make one public appearance each month.

Jayananda held up his hand, and the noise in the hall diminished. He muttered a few silent prayers, looked out at the audience and started his presentation.

He began by speaking for some twenty minutes on the theme of Shuddhadvaita, the philosophy of pure nondualism whereby even the everyday world of cause and effect, that glorious illusion often referred to in the Hindu scriptures as maya, is seen from the divine perspective as part of the one reality that encompasses all being. But in affirming the monistic view, he never negated the world of the senses. Rather, he focused on the underlying unity of dualism and monism, a position that eventually led him to the focal point of his presentation.

"Ultimately, everything, all reality, is found within the mind," he confidently asserted. "Past and future are in the mind. You can color the mind with any hue that you wish. It is like a piece of clean white cloth. Soak it in red dye and it will become red; soak it in blue dye and it will become blue. Do you not see that if you study mathematics, numbers will come easily to you, and if you study Sanskrit, the vocabulary of the pandit will be yours. In the same way, if you think good thoughts, the fruit thereof will be beneficial actions, whereas if your mind is blemished with bad intentions, only evil actions will result . . .

The mind is everything. By the mind, one is bound; by the mind, one is freed. If I think that I am enslaved, the fact that I live in a palace will not bring me freedom . . .

I am a child of Ma Tara. Who or what can bind me? When a scorpion bites you, if you affirm there is no venom in you, you will be cured. Similarly, one who knows with absolute certitude that he is free, is indeed free. The imbecile who can only think of himself as bound to this world, indeed becomes bound to this world."

Jayananda's theme remained the same, but now he started punctuating his discourse with melodic renderings of verses from renowned Hindu poet-saints. Soon he turned inward, lapsing into virtual stream-of-consciousness recitation of his own inner text, all the while keeping his audience enthralled with the power of his vision.

The tirthankara was nearing the culmination of his performance. He turned to parable, and at the end of one such story he drew his conclusion "The blossoms on the trees bounce and jiggle in the wind until the child thinks that they are living beings. But the grownups explain to the child that the blossoms are not moving of themselves. If the wind is removed, they will cease to move. Hence it is ignorance that posits the notion, 'I am the ultimate cause of my actions.' In truth all of our strength comes from Ma Tara. All is silent if she removes herself from us."

Jayananda had said enough. He made one final invocation to Ma Tara, arose from the pillow and joined the company of a number of his disciples who were preparing to escort him from the room. The crowd understood that the evening was over and inaugurated the same ritualistic chant that had christened the meeting. Jayananda responded by looking out into the sea of souls and bringing his palms together at his forehead. As he brought his hands back down to his side, the tirthankara's eyes caught sight of one of his disciples sitting next to two handsome young men in the front of the hall. One of the two boys particularly caught his attention. A feeling of exhilaration shot through his body. *Could it be*, he thought, *another Ram Das?* He would have to meet him—and soon.

Chapter 15

For several weeks after he had noticed Govinda sitting amongst the crowd at his monthly audience, Jayananda became incapable of giving any more than fleeting attention to his temple duties. The tirthankara failed to regularly attend the various daily puja offerings to Ma Tara in the temple sanctuary. During the times that he was supposed to be enlightening his students, he would often drift off into dream-like states of consciousness and fail to complete his presentations. The situation became so disconcerting to his disciples that several of them started to become worried about their guru's condition and reluctantly approached Manindra with their concerns. The temple owner finally brought the matter to Jayananda's attention, and the tirthankara knew that there was only one solution: he had to see the boy.

So it was that about one month after the cousins' excursion to the Ma Tara temple, Bhabanath found himself fervently trying to explain to Govinda what his friend, Hriday, had relayed to him about the tirthankara's wishes.

"I tell you, my little cousin, Hriday has made it abundantly clear to me that Shri Jayananda wants to meet you." Bhabanath could not keep his excitement hidden. "This is a blessing."

The young man attempted to quiet himself by carefully guiding a stream of water from an ornately designed ceramic pitcher into a small, brass drinking cup.

"And I know Hriday extremely well. He has been at the

temple for a number of years and is one of Shri Jayananda's closest and most devoted disciples. He would never lie, nor even attempt to stretch the truth, about such an important matter."

Bhabanath put the pitcher back down on the table. Govinda stretched his own cup in the direction of Bhabanath. A sudden flick of the wrist indicated that he likewise desired a refill. Bhabanath responded by unconsciously picking up the pitcher and directing its contents into Govinda's empty vessel.

"Hriday may have mistaken me for someone else. There were many people there that evening."

Bhabanath shook his head rapidly. "Even I noticed the way Shri Jayananda looked at you as he was leaving the hall. Don't tell me you were not aware of that stare. As I recall, your face became quite flushed."

"But why should Shri Jayananda want to meet with me?" Govinda ruminated aloud. "What in the world could I have done to deserve the attention of such a famous guru?" He raised the cup to his lips and slowly took in some of the cooling liquid.

Bhabanath shrugged his shoulders. "I am simply the messenger," he explained. "All I know is what Hriday has told me."

"Which is?"

"Which is, that when Shri Jayananda noticed you in his audience the other evening, he sensed an aura of highly developed spirituality emanating from your being, and that he would like to have you return to the temple and attend one of the sessions reserved for only his personal disciples."

Govinda temporarily interrupted the discussion to again quench his thirst. When he had emptied the cup of the last of its contents he firmly placed it down on the table and slowly rubbed his hairless chin with the extended fingers of his right hand. "May I be perfectly honest with you, Bhabanath?"

"Why not? Haven't we always been honest with each other, dear cousin," Bhabanath replied.

"Well, the truth is that I had a rather difficult time trying to understand many of the things Shri Jayananda was talking about that evening. I admit that I enjoyed his story about the child and the fluttering blossoms, and there was a certain beauty to his voice when he chanted his devotional songs, but his discussions of monism and dualism, attachment and detachment . . . well, it was, to say the least, rather confusing. So I must admit I am somewhat taken aback that he would say such a thing."

Bhabanath drummed his fingertips on the edge of the table and glanced at the ceiling. "Look Govinda," he said, again focusing his eyes on his cousin. "It was only a few weeks ago that you informed me you wanted to learn more about such matters. To my way of thinking, it seems that you have now been presented by fate with the perfect opportunity to fulfill your desires. If you accept this invitation, then I am certain you would be able to speak to Shri Jayananda directly. And what does it matter if you do not completely grasp such theological abstractions as Shuddhadvaita, Brahman, maya, nirgun, or sagun? If the truth were told, I would seriously doubt that many of Shri Jayananda's closest and most learned disciples could even understand what he is talking about."

Govinda calmly pushed his chair back and stood up. He squeezed his hands together, turned around, and methodically paced across the floor to the opposite wall.

Bhabanath waited for his cousin's reaction by pouring himself yet another cup of water.

"There is another problem," Govinda announced at last. "I don't think my father would approve of such a meeting."

Bhabanath rolled his eyes. "I do not mean to sound disrespectful, but I fail to see what your father's opinion has to do with any of this. It is not as if you are going to suddenly get up and leave his household to become one of Shri Jayananda's permanent disciples. Remember, you have merely been invited by Shri Jayananda to come to the temple to meet with him. And quite frankly, I don't see why your father even has to know about it."

Govinda came back to the table. He did not sit down but stood with his hands leaning lightly against the top of the wooden surface. "Perhaps you are right," he said. His words were once again filled with their former vitality. "After all, it is not as if I am still a young child. In just a few months, I will celebrate my nineteenth birthday."

Bhabanath stretched his arm across the table and firmly took hold of Govinda's empty cup. He stood up and walked to the near corner of the room where a large, metallic bowl that was already half-filled with a goodly number of used plates and utensils sat awaiting the servant's attention. He added the two vessels to the collection and returned to his chair.

"I will be seeing Hriday later in the afternoon. I can tell him to go ahead and arrange the meeting with Shri Jayananda if you like."

Govinda remained mute.

"Well?"

"I guess there can be no harm in meeting him," Govinda reluctantly admitted. "But there is one last thing, Bhabanath."

"And what is that?

"I would like you to come with me."

Bhabanath frowned. "Listen to you," he exclaimed. "You have just now told me that you are no longer a child, and then you immediately act like one. If Shri Jayananda had wanted to meet both of us, I am quite sure he would have said so. I am afraid that this is something you are going to have to do on your own."

Govinda felt foolish and asked himself why he hadn't thought before he spoke. "Once again, you are right, dear cousin. Yes, you can go ahead and tell Hriday that I am interested in attending such a meeting."

"It is as good as done," proclaimed Bhabanath. "I will ask Hriday whether Shri Jayananda has a certain date and time in mind. Hopefully, I will be able to let you know the answer by early this evening."

"Thank you," Govinda sighed.

"Think nothing of it."

Bhabanath went to the mirror and started to slick back his hair. "This is a rare opportunity which should not be missed."

"I hope you are right," Govinda whispered beneath his breath.

Chapter 16

Jayananda sat motionless in the lotus position. There was no one else with him in the small, grassy grove that sat atop the swollen knoll alongside the Ganges. The morning sky was cloudless, and the air had a cold bite to it. The tirthankara's eyes were closed, but the puffy and swollen skin beneath them could not conceal their secret.

"Oh Ma," Jayananda loudly lamented, "Why do I remain so agitated? Why cannot my mind remain steadfast? Why do I long for him so? And why, O Ma, does he not come? Why does the beautiful one tarry? I know this grove has been sprinkled with dust from the sacred sites of Brindavan. Does that then mean that those who worship here must experience the agony of separation? Oh why does he stay away?"

Tears filled the corners of his closed eyelids. "Now I know how the loyal Sita felt when she was carried away from her lord Rama. Now I understand what it was like for the gopi Chandravali when she learned her beloved Krishna had abandoned her."

The tears readily turned into sobs. " O Ma, who is this boy with whom you torture my soul. Please tell me!"

Jayananda brought his hands to his head and covered his ears. For an extended period he repeated Ma Tara's name. Each time that the divine appellation left his quivering lips, his entire body swayed rhythmically from side to side. Increasingly he began to know a soothing warmth centered just above his tailbone. The glowing heat remained stationary for some time before it slowly made its way along his spine and into the

TARA'S SECRET 103

upper regions of his back and shoulders. For a while the flow of vitality paused. It seemed to linger in the middle of his neck, but it soon proceeded to the apex of his spine until it entered his head. Its final resting spot was a point just behind the tirthankara's forehead.

"Ma," Jayananda cried out in anticipatory joy, "O Ma, is it you?"

The heat soon transformed itself into a glowing white light which continued to grow in intensity until its brilliance nearly overwhelmed him. Then Jayananda heard what he was waiting and hoping for: the resonant sound of Ma Tara's voice in his ear. "Be assured, my son, that without separation there can be no joy. The taste of honey is that much sweeter when it is not consumed daily."

"But why does the mere thought of this boy cause me such anxiety?" the tirthankara inquired of the goddess. "I have not asked for his sweetness, and yet now that I have seen him, I cannot escape the desire."

"This boy is none other than an incarnation of a venerable agnivesha, a descendent of the god Agni who has yet again taken physical form to help reduce the suffering of souls in the world of samsara. You are to guide him. You must teach him the mystical truths that this world of lila has caused him to forget."

"But I do not feel worthy of such a charge," Jayananda cried.

"Do not fret. You will be guided. I am a devoted mother who is never far away from her children. You will accomplish your task."

Then she was gone.

At the same time that Jayananda was preoccupied in his revelatory ecstasy, Govinda met Hriday in front of the Ma Tara temple's main gate. From there, he was briskly guided to a nearby building that was normally used for religious celebrations.

Govinda entered the building and was astonished to see his escort immediately depart the premises undeclared. He was also surprised to find that the room's interior was empty of both persons and furniture. He stood alone and pondered what he should do next. He had just about convinced himself that the visit was a mistake, and that he should leave the compound to return home, when Jayananda unexpectedly made his appearance from a narrow doorway directly across from where he was standing.

Govinda watched the tirthankara approach. He could see that Jayananda's hair was standing on end, and that his eyes were red and swollen. In his left hand he carried a powdery-white, sweet meat, and in his right a small yellow tube rose.

Jayananda was only a few feet away from his guest. He slowed his pace and stopped. "These gifts are for you, my dear Govinda." He extended both objects in the direction of the young man.

Govinda looked down at the offerings and then back up at Jayananda. "I cannot take these," he replied matter of factly.

Jayananda dropped heavily to his knees and let out a deep and agonizing cry. "I have been waiting so long for you to come," he groaned. "Why is it that when you finally arrive you treat me so? Have you completely forgotten?"

Govinda was visibly shaken. He had not expected such a dramatic encounter, and the intensity of Jayananda's voice caused him to instinctively pull away. He backed up several steps, regained his balance, and stared down in a state of disbelief at the tirthankara.

Govinda was given little time to think. Jayananda bolted to his feet, cast the flower on the floor and thrust the sweet-meat into his hand. The tirthankara fell back down to the ground and bellowed: "Do not flee from me, my Rama; I will more than comfort you. Oh, stay my sly Krishna; do not leave me alone in Brindavan." Then he quieted himself and began to sing in a sweet and melodious voice:

> "I must go, he sings,
> In spite of your longing cries.
> Despite my passionate pleas,
> He says he must go.

He takes a half step back,
And then turns around to gaze
At this miserable heart.
I suffer joyfully,
Only hoping for his return.
Tell me,
Tell me my beautiful one,
Why do my limbs appear numb?
Why do my lips tremble
And my eyes well up with tears
While your gaze
Is silent?"

The last line of the poem had hardly left Jayananda's lips when he stood up, reached out swiftly with his left hand, and clutched hold of Govinda's arm. Govinda's reflexive reaction was to pull away, but the instant that the tirthankara touched his skin he felt a powerful wave of energy start flowing down into his hands and upward into his shoulders. It quickly spread throughout his entire body and negated any effort he might have made to pull himself free. It was one of the most pleasant feelings he had ever experienced. A super-heightened degree of physical sensitivity had combined with a deep and vivid reminiscence of maternal warmth. He could only stand there, almost helpless, and soak in the overwhelming sensations.

Jayananda let go of Govinda's limb and smiled. Almost immediately the joyous feelings left the young man to be replaced by a profound foreboding. It seemed to Govinda that he had suddenly been cast adrift on a perilous ocean. He looked into Jayananda's eyes. They had a transparency that caused him to look away.

"Do you not understand how long and how patiently I have been waiting for you, my dear Govinda?" the tirthankara repeated.

Govinda's fear was now in complete control of his will. He dropped the sweetmeat on the floor and ran out of the room. Behind him he could hear Jayananda's siren song calling him to return.

Chapter 17

Tell me, Govinda, why is it you are not eating any of your food this evening? You have hardly touched a single one of the dishes on your plate, even your chipatti remains half-eaten. It would seem you are practicing to become a sadhu."

Govinda looked across the table. "No, father, I can assure you that I have no plans to starve myself. I just do not feel hungry."

Mahendralal Narayan was a rotund man whose large brown eyes and greying mustache dominated his full face. "Well then, I am afraid you are going to cause our loyal Mukhdevi to think you are no longer enamored of her cooking."

Govinda cast his eyes down at his plate and shook his head. "It has nothing whatsoever to do with Mukhdevi's cooking, father. It is really quite simple. As I said, I have no appetite—no more, no less."

"And why is that my son?" Mahendralal inquired after consuming a vegetable-filled portion of chipatti and licking his fingers. "Are you not feeling well? Perhaps we need to contact Dr. Mukerjee."

"That will not be necessary," Govinda replied. "Physically, I am fine. I just have a lot on my mind at the moment."

"Ah, you are referring to law school." Mahendralal dipped a fresh piece of ghi-soaked chipatti into a small metal cup filled with spicy lentil soup. "I was just telling your mother earlier this afternoon that I have recently been in written correspondence with my cousin who lives in Bombay. He suggests very strongly that you consider taking your degree in England. Not only does it take less time to complete the course there, but the prestige of an English law degree will be greatly beneficial when you return to India and start your own practice."

"But he is much too young to be going overseas," interjected Sarvani. "Just think of all the dangers he might encounter, not to mention the problem of pollution."

Govinda's mother was a domineering looking woman whose hefty stature almost matched that of her husband. Her once attractive figure was now hidden behind rolls of flaccid flesh, and her classical features had long since given way to gravity and wrinkles.

"Nonsense," grumbled Mahendralal. "The boy is almost nineteen years old. In fact, he is no longer a boy but a young man, and in any case, he will not be completely alone. My sister's in-laws have family who live in London."

"It was your own sister who told me that in England it is almost impossible for a young man to avoid meat, not to mention the other temptations." Sarvani lifted her bowl to her mouth and drained it of the last vestiges of lentil soup.

Mahendralal waited until she had returned the container to the table. "No doubt Indrani was exaggerating, as usual," he said.

"But what about the caste elders?" Sarvani persisted. "As you well know, there is a caste prohibition against traveling across the seas. If Govinda were to go to England, they would certainly outcast him. How such a disgrace would add to his professional prestige, I find very difficult to imagine."

Mahendralal ignored Sarvani's sarcastic tone. "You can leave the caste elders to me," he calmly asserted. "I know these men, and I can assure you there is nothing a few rupees and a purification ritual or two cannot cure." He reached toward the center of the table for yet another chipatti.

"Since there are many good law schools in India, including several of the best right here in Benares, I do not see why, for a little sahib prestige, Govinda should be forced by his father to leave his family and go traipsing off to England." A hint of anger was now present in Sarvani's words.

Mahendralal began to lose his patience. He looked scornfully at his wife. "It is not a question of forcing the boy to leave home," he said. "In this regard I am a modern man. I believe that the decision should be left up to him, but that he should not be unduly influenced." He looked sternly at Sarvani who did not bother to return his glance.

Govinda had heard enough of his parents' bickering for one evening. "Excuse me, father," he curtly interrupted. "If you do not mind, I would like to ask your permission to leave the table. I am tired."

Mahendralal readily acknowledged Govinda's request. "Certainly, my son," he answered, "but make sure that you do not go overly long without eating. As you can see, your mother constantly worries about you." Once more the man looked derisively at his wife. "I will instruct Mukhdevi to make sure she leaves out some fresh chipattis, dal, and vegetables for you in the kitchen. Tomorrow I will mention your symptoms to Dr. Mukerjee."

Govinda did not bother to respond to Mahendralal's last remark. Instead, he ritualistically thanked his father, bid his mother well, and quietly left the table.

He went directly to his room and hurled himself onto his cot. He lay there for some time and just stared at the ceiling. Images and impressions of the past few days flitted in and out of consciousness. He decided that he should try to clear his mind of all thoughts. He concentrated as best he could on the sound of the word 'Om.'

Jayananda's face would not leave him. But even more powerful than the tirthankara's ever-present mental portrait were the ambivalent feelings attached to it. On the one hand, Govinda wanted to rid himself of Jayananda's image, and yet there was also present an underlying and alluring wish to stare directly into the tirthankara's eyes and see more clearly. *If father only knew*, he thought to himself. He sat up.

He got to his feet and crossed the room. On his desk sat a

new edition of the great Indian epic, the *Ramayana*, which Bhabanath had recently loaned him. It was perhaps the most popular tale in all of India, and Govinda was aware of the major contours of characterization and plot, yet he had never actually read the classic, primarily because Mahendralal had seen to it that from an early age his son read mainly selections from English literature.

Govinda picked up the volume from the desktop, tucked it firmly under his arm, and came back to his charpoi. He again reclined, positioned himself comfortably, and began to rapidly thumb through the text's copious pages. He stopped here and there trying to get a flavor of its format and style.

Near the end of his perusal Govinda arrived at a scene in one of the latter chapters where the avatar-hero, Rama, was just about to dispatch the wicked demon Ravana. For some reason his eyes focused on the following passage:

> Rama, reminded by the words of Matali, took his flaming arrow like a hissing snake. He spoke a mantra upon it as the Vedas ordain. The strong one placed in his bow that great and mighty arrow. Enraged, he fiercely bent his bow against Ravana, and intent on his mark, he shot the entrail-tearing arrow. Bearing the death of the body, the arrow flew with great speed and tore through the heart of the evil-working Ravana. Then, red with his blood and rapid, that arrow, destroyer of bodies, robbing the life-breath of Ravana, drove into the face of the earth. Swiftly struck from his hand, his bow and his arrow dropped with his life breath upon the ground. Unbreathing, with awful speed, the glorious lord of the demons fell from his chariot to earth, like Vitra stuck by the thunderbolt.

Govinda closed the book and set it down on the bed beside him. Once more he stared off into space. *Good versus evil*, he whispered to himself. *Why is it that so many religious stories are filled with the themes of good versus evil or righteousness versus injustice? Is life really so simple as depicted here? Is it always a matter of black and white?* He was too exhausted to answer his own question. He closed his eyes and let the world slip slowly away.

Sometime during the middle of the night, or perhaps in

the wee hours of the morning, the mental gymnastics in which Govinda's subconscious mind had been continually engaged coalesced into a vivid dream. He found himself in an long hallway surrounded by countless bodiless heads that were all screaming at him to do different things. One of the largest faces kept directing him towards a large boat that lay anchored in an adjacent room. Another offered him two strands of rope and told him to tie his hands together, while a third kept wanting him to join a nearby wedding celebration.

In the midst of this chaos, there appeared at one end of the passage a golden chariot driven by a figure who had the body of a warrior and a featureless head. Govinda became frightened of the figure and tried to run away, but the more effort he made, the closer the phantom came. Unexpectedly the figure divided itself in two. Soon both of the new faceless creatures were preparing to fight with one another. In the ensuing battle, both periodically turned to him with the same repetitious cry: "Do not run, Govinda; I will protect you."

At last, the bigger of the two took out a long, black, jewel-studded sword and swiftly decapitated his opponent. Then the figure turned triumphantly back towards Govinda and began showering him with lotus petals. "O ancient one, you have been sent here to worship and be worshipped by means of the secret door," it announced.

The dream haunted Govinda. *Who were these phantoms*, he kept asking himself, *and what did they represent?* Over the following days he speculated that they were merely products of the mental residue accumulated in the canyons of his mind after reading the last section of the Ramayana. But some part of him was not completely convinced that this was the entire story.

Govinda's background and education shunned superstition. Nevertheless, as he became increasingly unnerved he contemplated seeing a brahman who specialized in the art of divination, and when he next saw his cousin, he mentioned this to him. Bhabanath in turn suggested that the person Govinda should contact was an old family friend who knew practically every soothsayer and astrologer in Benares. After another day of meticulously weighing and measuring the pros and cons of such a move, Govinda finally surrendered to his inquisitiveness and asked Bhabanath to arrange a meeting.

It took some days before Bhabanath could contact the brahman, and by the time Govinda heard that an appointment had been organized, he was no longer certain he wanted to go ahead with the arrangement. He realized, however, that to back out now would put Bhabanath in an embarrassing situation. Had the man not maintained such a close relationship with the family, a cancellation might not have created any great difficulty. Such was not the case. Consequently, Govinda accepted the fruits of his actions and diligently made preparations to follow through with the plan.

The evening before his scheduled visit was to take place Govinda took out the piece of wrinkled brown paper on which Bhabanath had written a set of directions. He looked down at the man's name. *Swami Ramananda*, he read to himself. He tried to envision what the swami might look like, but the only image entering his mind was that of the tirthankara.

Chapter 18

Govinda deftly navigated his way through the seeming labyrinth of long, narrow alleyways. The swami's quarters were situated in a small neighborhood dominated by tea stalls and cloth shops. From the Ganges it was a short but steep uphill walk to the large front door.

Govinda initiated a series of rhythmic knocks on the stained wooden surface. He was breathing heavily. His rap was answered by a young, barefooted servant who cautiously peeped through the crack in the door before opening it fully and inviting him into a surprisingly large room. The space was filled with countless stone and brass icons from the Hindu pantheon. Govinda was particularly taken with an immense statue of Ganesh who held in his fully extended trunk a polished black steel sword. He had seen countless depictions of the elephant-headed god, but never one of him bearing such a weapon.

Swami Ramananda entered the room. He was a tall, thin, frail-looking man whose freshly pressed white turban appeared to be too large for his narrow head. Govinda noticed that his thumbs were continually moving back and forth across the insides of his fingers. He introduced himself to his guest and then went straight to the point. "I understand that you are in search of someone who can interpret a dream," he said.

Govinda made an affirmative motion with his head. "That

is correct. I believe my friend Bhabanath contacted you."

"Actually, it was Bhabanath's father who contacted me," the man replied. "We grew up together near Lucknow, but that is really of no importance to you." The swami stopped several feet away from Govinda and carefully adjusted his turban with the palms of his hands.

Now that Swami Ramananda was closer, Govinda could see that his hands were permanently gnarled by arthritis. The swami must have observed his guest's glance. "One of the pleasantries of old age," he uttered without hesitation.

Govinda felt awkward and did not know what to say, but the swami relieved him of his difficulty by gesturing to a nearby cushioned chair. "You can sit here," he said.

Govinda followed his instructions.

"There are a good many soothsayers to be found in this city. Some are very skilled; some are charlatans. In order for me to guide you appropriately, it is of paramount importance that I know the contents of your dream. You see, dream interpretation is specialized, and the area of expertise is based on the nature of the dream's contents."

Govinda recounted his dream. He took care to describe every incident with as much detail as he could remember.

The swami kept his eyes firmly fixed on the boy. Intermittently during the retelling he would slowly nod his head up and down.

"I believe I know the man who can best interpret this dream for you."

Govinda waited expectantly for Swami Ramananda to disclose the name of his chosen soothsayer.

"There is a certain young guru, some call him a tirthankara, presently associated with the Ma Tara temple who, despite his tender years, has become renowned throughout Benares for his interpretations of dreams related to the avatars Rama and Krishna . . . And what is more, he is well-known for his purity of soul, which is always important in these matters. His name is Shri Jayananda. You may have heard of him?"

Govinda closed his eyes and tilted his chin down towards his chest. He breathed deeply.

Swami Ramananda was taken by his visitor's rather peculiar response. "Is there something wrong, my boy?" he asked. " If you are worried about getting an audience, I can certainly see to that."

"No, I was just thinking about something you said," Govinda lied.

"And what was that?"

The young man regained his composure. "You mentioned that this guru was known for his interpretations of dreams related to Rama and Krishna?"

"That is correct," the swami confirmed.

"I may sound ignorant, swamiji, but I don't see how my dream has anything to do with the two avatars."

The swami rocked his head back and forth. "As I am sure you are aware, dreams are essentially secret codes. They make use of certain symbols whose meanings the dreamer does not always grasp. It will be up to Shri Jayananda to tell you the specifics of your dream, but I have had enough experience to see that many of your dream symbols are related to the avatars."

"Some people claim that Shri Jayananda is slightly mad," Govinda said, hoping that his comment would elicit further appraisal from the swami.

"All gurus and soothsayers are slightly mad," the swami affirmed. "That is why they are capable of interpreting dreams . . . Some even say that madness is the doorway to knowledge."

A sense of unease prevented Govinda from pursuing the theme. "I will need some time to think this matter through," he said, abruptly changing the topic. I greatly appreciate your taking your valuable time to give me advice. Now, how much do I owe you?"

Swami Ramananda raised his bent hand into the air and shook his head from side to side. "For a friend of Bhabanath's, there is no charge," he said.

Govinda wanted to protest but realized that the swami would not change his mind. "You are most kind," was his only reply.

The swami simply nodded his head.

Govinda knew it was time to depart. He placed his hands

together at his mouth and bowed to the accompanying sound of "Namaskar."

Swami Ramananda returned the gesture. "Namaskar."

The servant was called to escort the guest to the door. As he waited for the boy's arrival Govinda remembered the statue of Ganesh. "Oh, one more thing swamiji. If you don't mind, I have another question."

The swami let his hands drop to the sides of his legs. "Of course," he agreed. "What do you want to know?"

"I have never before seen a representation of Ganesh with a sword held in his trunk." Govinda dramatically gestured in the direction of the massive elephant. "And I was just wondering whether this specific depiction of the god might have any secret, symbolic significance?"

The muscles in the swami's face tightened ever so slightly. "Yes, it was a very rare and important find. As you probably know, according to the myth, Ganesh's father, Shiva, cut off his son's head with a sword and then replaced it with the head of an elephant. So this is the head-severing sword."

The man walked up to the statue and brushed the sword with the back of his hand. "But the sculptor who conceived and created this image told me that the reason Ganesh is grasping the weapon in his trunk is that it is the son's secret desire to in turn cut off his father's head."

Govinda transgressed his pledge. "And what do you think of that interpretation swamiji?"

The swami's answer was not evasive. "Some part in all of us wants to kill our fathers," he bluntly stated, "and some part in all of our fathers wants to kill us."

Govinda was intrigued by the swami's analysis, but the servant was now standing at his side. He made another bow, repeated his farewells and allowed the boy to escort him from the room.

On his way home Govinda's mind was pulled by contradictory impulses. One feeling told him to rush straight to Jayananda and have his dream immediately explained. He wanted to again feel the enchanting sensation of the tirthankara's magical touch. But then his will pulled back.

There was too much strangeness there, too much that was foreign to his nature. He should forget the whole episode and follow his father's advice by finding a good law school. Yes, perhaps London would be the answer. He could leave home and experience a new adventure while at the same time prepare himself for a practical future.

Govinda arrived at the house and headed straight for his room. "Is everything all right?" his mother asked as he hurriedly passed her by.

"Yes, everything is fine, Mother," he shouted before he closed the door. He went to the desk, pushed aside the *Ramayana* and picked up John Locke's, *Two Treatises on Government.* He had made his decision. He would forget all about this strange tirthankara.

Govinda was standing alone in the courtyard of the Ma Tara temple. His promise to forget about Jayananda had been short-lived. Something inside him kept wondering whether he had not been overly hasty in making his decision, and after another lengthy day of protracted agonizing over the problem, he concluded that only a second meeting would completely resolve the issue. His plan was to wait for Jayananda near the entryway to the main temple since he was reasonably sure that the tirthankara would go there at least once during the afternoon hours.

Only a handful of minutes had passed when Govinda noticed Hriday hurrying in his direction. "Shri Jayananda wants to see you at once," the disciple loudly attested from the distance.

Hriday slowed his pace and stopped. Govinda closely examined the messenger. The man was fidgeting with his hands and appeared anxious to get going. "But how did Shri Jayananda know that I was here?" Govinda asked.

"Shri Jayananda knows many things," Hriday retorted. "Now we must go."

Govinda responded to the command by following the man across the courtyard and into the hidden precincts of the temple grounds.

The question he had asked Hriday remained lodged in his mind. *How could he have known? Did he possess some type of telepathic power? It was more likely that one of the disciples had reported his whereabouts to Shri Jayananda, but only Hriday knew his appearance.* Govinda understood he had to let the speculations go. There would be no immediate answer. More significantly, nervousness at the thought of once again meeting with the tirthankara had started to mask any other concern.

They arrived at the same building where Govinda had previously met with Jayananda. Hriday swiftly left the scene without comment. This time, however, Jayananda made an almost instantaneous appearance on the porch. The tirthankara looked calm and subdued as if he had expected his guest's arrival. Govinda in turn seemed almost mesmerized by the apparition. Whereas on the former occasion he had been filled with anxiety, now he only knew a sense of heightened anticipation.

"Come, let us walk," Shri Jayananda said.

The tirthankara strode rapidly across the grass. Govinda found himself virtually running in order to keep up.

Jayananda's course led toward the river's edge. From there, the two men walked silently along the Ganges' bank for some distance until they arrived at a small house surrounded by a quaint garden. Jayananda indicated with his left hand that the building was their destination. "This is the residence of one of the temple householders," he said. "I often come here. The surroundings remind me very much of the village where I grew up."

The tirthankara proceeded across the garden and entered into one of the house's outer rooms. Govinda tracked close behind

"What do you mean by 'householder'?" Govinda asked when they were inside.

"The gentleman generously supports the community, but he is not a disciple. He is a family man who has taken no vows."

Jayananda walked over to a far window. He peered out into the garden. "You have had a dream," he pronounced.

Govinda was taken by surprise. "Yes," he mumbled.

Jayananda turned around. His eyes had become glazed and

a haunting smile spread across his face. Govinda noticed the change. His own mood began to shift. Doubts began to creep back into his consciousness. *Why did I come?* he thought. Meanwhile Jayananda had started to slowly come towards him. "It was a very unusual dream," Govinda stuttered. He hoped that his words would ward off the man's approach.

"I know," Jayananda replied.

The tirthankara placed both of his hands just below Govinda's neck and looked into his eyes. The moment Jayananda touched him, a surge of energy inundated Govinda's entire body. This was the same feeling he had experienced during their earlier meeting, except this time Jayananda did not let go but kept his hands firmly placed on the young man's shoulders. Before Govinda knew it, the entire room seemed to spin inward. Waves of delight crashed down on him as if he were some isolated beach about to become engulfed by an oceanic presence whose nature words could not even come close to describing. Everything became momentarily blurry. Only the eerie echoes of the tirthankara's laugh remained . . . Govinda slipped into unconsciousness.

When the young man regained his awareness, Jayananda was standing over him. The tirthankara passed his hand back and forth above Govinda's chest. On his face there remained a serene smile.

"What happened?" Govinda asked. The grogginess in his voice indicated that he was still somewhat dazed by the incident.

"You experienced Ma," Jayananda replied.

The tirthankara reached down and gently stroked Govinda's hair. Govinda responded by looking up at the master's face with the longing of an abandoned child.

"And you told me something," Jayananda continued. "You told me that you were not your mother's son."

Govinda's face sank.

"Do not worry," Jayananda said. "It is not what you think, for you are also not your father's son. Like me, you belong to Ma Tara. You want to be close to your real mother, and she wants her son to reside near to her."

During his walk home Govinda replayed these words in his head. He sensed that somehow his life would never be the same. Little did he suspect, however, that when he reached his destination he would be greeted with the news that his father was dead.

Chapter 19

Govinda awaited Bhabanath's arrival. Now and again he would take a sip of tea from the earthen cup that rested on the table next to him, but he hardly noticed the owner of the tea stall nor the numerous customers who came and went. His mind was preoccupied with formulating a convincing presentation for the news he would soon convey to his cousin.

The six months that had gone by since the spreading of his father's ashes had given Govinda time to quietly contemplate his own future. According to custom he was still in a period of mourning, and should therefore not have made any significant life decisions, but in this matter he had abandoned tradition and determined the new course his life would take. He knew it would not be easy explaining his choice to the family. At least with Bhabanath he felt there would be a sense of understanding, if not agreement.

"Would you like more?" asked the owner. He pointed his bony finger in the direction of Govinda's cup.

The question startled Govinda. It took him a moment to reorient himself. When he answered, it was with a brief wave of his hand.

The gesture brought the man scurrying to the table. Govinda watched him fill his cup to overflowing with the mocha-colored liquid. "You like the tea?" the owner asked as he completed his task.

"Your tea is excellent," Govinda replied. "It is nice and sweet. Just the way I like it."

A look of pleasure crossed the man's face. He bowed and retreated in the direction of another customer.

Govinda had almost emptied his second cup when Bhabanath made his appearance. "So sorry to be late," the cousin exclaimed. He hurriedly took a seat next to Govinda and waved vigorously in the direction of the owner. "I was visiting an old friend and completely forgot about the time."

"Time is the one thing I have plenty of," said Govinda.

The owner arrived with Bhabanath's tea. "Would you like a sweet today?" he asked the newcomer.

"Tea is enough," said Bhabanath. He lifted the cup to his lips, took a healthy sip, and placed it on the table.

"You know, Govinda, I doubt our mothers would not approve of this place. Even though it is owned and run by brahmans, I am certain that they would find it impure. I can just hear my mother now: 'Bhabanath, how can you even imagine putting to your lips a cup that does not come from your own household? Who knows where in the world it has been or who has touched it?'" The high pitch of his voice added to the mockery.

Govinda laughed.

"But you did not invite me here to speak of food taboos," Bhabanath switched directions. "What is on your mind?"

Govinda swallowed hard. He could feel his body begin to tighten. All of his planned explanations seemed to disappear into the nether regions of his mind. He froze. "Well," he slowly began, hoping that his ideas would return to him as he started to speak, "I just wanted, . . . I just wanted to let you know about a very important decision I have recently made and the reasons for making it."

Bhabanath gently pushed his cup towards the center of the table and swiveled his chair in Govinda's direction.

"I, . . . I have decided to become a disciple of Shri Jayananda."

"What do you mean, disciple?" Bhabanath inquired. He cocked his head slightly in one direction and lowered his eyebrows.

Govinda shifted his gaze downward. " What I mean is that I plan on taking my vows," he responded in a sudden burst.

"You cannot be serious," said Bhabanath. "Your father's ashes have hardly been scattered and you decide to abandon the world? I think you know that this is not what he would have wanted?"

"Yes, I know that father would have wanted me to be admitted to the bar, but . . . I have given the issue a great deal of thought, Bhabanath, and to be very honest, a life dedicated to the law does not appeal to my heart. You see, I have come to the conclusion that the life of renunciation is my calling."

Bhabanath lifted his cupped hands in front of his mouth and tapped his fingers. "Have you told your mother?" he asked "No, not yet."

"Have you given any thought to how she might feel about such a decision? You are her only living son, you know."

Jayananda's words regarding Ma Tara flashed into Govinda's mind, and his initial reaction was to tell Bhabanath that yes, he was her only son, but that she was not his only mother. He abstained, however, and replied with a more conventional answer. "Frankly, I think she will be much more understanding than father would have been."

Bhabanath dropped his hands to the table and leaned forward. "It is he, isn't it? It is Shri Jayananda."

"What do you mean?"

Bhabanath again leaned back in his chair and raised his left hand to his chin. "My meaning is this, dear cousin. It is not so much the life of renunciation that you want. What you really desire is to be with Shri Jayananda."

Govinda sensed the bite of cynicism in Bhabanath's words. He tried to remain calm. "I believe that Shri Jayananda can teach me many things about the path of renunciation, if that is what you mean," he said.

"Well, that may be, Govinda, but from our previous conversations I can easily perceive that there is much more to the matter than that. It is not difficult to see that this guru, Shri Jayananda, has grabbed something deep inside of you, something that you both long for and fear at the same time."

"Of course he has great spiritual power," Govinda shot back. "I will not deny that, but you speak as if I need a new father."

Bhabanath removed his hand from his chin, turned his palms upward, and widened his eyes. "Those are your words," he said.

Govinda shook his head. The muscles in the side of his face pulled back. "I know that it might be difficult for people to understand," he said, "but it is something I must do. I cannot live my life as a charade."

Bhabanath smiled. "You have always had a will of your own," he asserted. "Even when we were little, you always got your way."

"And you have always been one for exaggeration, dear cousin."

Bhabanath reached over and put his hand on Govinda's arm. "Of course I will support you. I just hope that your mother will not be overly pained. Two deaths in one year might be more than she could manage."

"Mother is stronger than you think," said Govinda. "And, in any case, I am not going into seclusion. The temple will be my new home but not my cloister."

"I wish you well then, Govinda."

After he had departed the tea stall Bhabanath could not help but recall that he had been the one who first encouraged his cousin to meet Shri Jayananda. *Would I have done the same had I known it would lead to this?* he silently asked himself.

He knew there was no answer. Destiny had its own way with mortals.

Chapter 20

The disciples sat lotus-style in a large semi-circle. All eighteen young men were dressed in loosely hung orange robes. Their backs were all perfectly straight, and each one of their heads was so closely shaven that only a very slight dullness from atop their skulls gave any indication that the skin was any different from that found on their foreheads. Their eyes were lightly shut, and their hands were gently held together between their knees.

Seated directly in front of them, lost in a meditative trance, was Jayananda. He wore only a white loincloth accompanied by a thin cotton sash that dangled lazily from his left shoulder before culminating in a small bundle in his lap. The hair on his head was also closely cropped, but enough stubble remained to almost match the growth of his short beard and mustache.

Govinda opened his eyes and looked hazily out at the tirthankara. He was constantly amazed at the length of time Jayananda could remain in a state of deep meditation. His own ability to maintain this psychic condition was woefully lacking. After nearly two years of periodic daily efforts, he could now focus his mind on his mantra for fairly-extended periods of time, but regardless of how sustained his effort, there always seemed to be some point when abiding mental images started to slowly leak back into his consciousness.

Jayananda soon opened his own eyes and briefly scanned the faces of his students. He clapped his hands together twice.

The loud, sharp sounds immediately recaptured the disciples' attention. "Now let us speak of the vital psychic powers," he said.

The disciples focused intently on their guru and awaited his discourse.

"What is the mind?" Jayananda asked.

Normally the tirthankara would expect an answer from one of the disciples, but today he was impatient. "It is a three-fold manifestation composed of intellect, ego, and the perceptual faculties," he said without waiting for a response. "It is this mind that is the receptacle for the effects of karma, the residue left by action that forms habit patterns."

Jayananda briefly looked for signs of the disciples' understanding.

"And how does the functioning of this mind take place?"

Again, the guru's question was rhetorical. He proceeded to immediately provide his mesmerized listeners with the desired answer: "The functioning of the mind takes place through a number of fluctuations that give form to the perceptions, thoughts, and emotions . . .

What are these fluctuations? We call them valid understanding, error, imagination, sleep, and memory. How is it that these fluctuations find a state of unity? They find a state of unity through that which we identify as 'I.' That is, all perceptions and thoughts arise because of the sense of individual self."

Jayananda reached out and roughly plucked a number of blades of grass with his fingers. He raised his hand high above his head and cast the grass into the air. The various pieces soon separated and began floating in a variety of directions. When all of the blades had finally settled to the ground, he returned to his lesson.

"What is this 'I'? This 'I' is like these blades of grass containing no real foundation. Thus, like these blades, it is blown hither and dither by the whimsical winds of time and place. What do we call this 'I'? We call it conventional consciousness. What is the product of this conventional consciousness? It is the generator and perpetuator of ceaseless patterns. And by what name do we call these ceaseless patterns? We call them samsara, the endless whirl of pain and pleasure that is existence."

How many of them have the insight to really grasp what I am saying? Jayananda thought to himself as he again inspected the faces of the disciples. *Perhaps only Hriday, Vaikuntha, and Govinda. Yes, Govinda understands. It is his nature to understand, but the others?*

"And how do we categorize this conventional consciousness? We categorize it as the unenlightened mind. Why do we categorize it as the unenlightened mind? Because this consciousness is fraught with afflictions."

Jayananda breathed deeply and slowed the pace of his delivery. "What is the source of these afflictions?" he asked.

The tirthankara returned to his conventional style. He ceased answering his own questions and waited for a response.

"And what is the source of these afflictions?" he repeated. "Tell me, O enlightened ones, O children of Ma Tara, what is it that forms the source of these afflictions?"

"Ignorance," said Govinda.

Jayananda had guessed Govinda would be the one to respond. He looked directly at his star pupil. "And what then, Govinda, is the nature of this ignorance?"

Most of the disciples would have cast their eyes downward in the face of such a direct encounter with the tirthankara, but Govinda did not flinch. Rather, he returned the gaze. "This ignorance comes into being because of mistaken identity," he answered. His tone was powerful and unswerving.

Govinda's demeanor pleased Jayananda, but the tirthankara gave no outward indication of his approval. "And what is the nature of this mistake?"

"The nature of this mistake is the taking of the non-eternal to be the eternal, the taking of the impure to be the pure, the taking of discomfort to be pleasure and the taking of the non-self to be the self." With each answer, Govinda's sense of inner power became magnified.

Jayananda nodded his head. He knew that Govinda had grasped, as others could not, the deeper spiritual meaning of the words he had so accurately articulated, but in his heart the tirthankara was also growing tired of such lessons. Were it not for the fact that Manindra demanded that each year he train a certain number of new disciples in the knowledge of the Vedanta, he would not have spent so much time in the outer circle. He had recently thought of telling the temple owner that he no longer wished to be its spokesman, but he also realized that this was impossible. *If only Harish were still alive*, he thought.

Images of his beloved Harish started to filter into his consciousness, and with them there came an almost supernatural sense of his closeness. It was as if the former temple owner had suddenly reappeared and whispered in his ear that he should put aside the standard formulas and follow his inner voice.

Yes, that is what's needed, Jayananda mused. He could feel a new surge of energy welling up within him.

"That is enough for today," he abruptly announced to the disciples. "It is time to offer your puja to Ma Tara."

The disciples mechanically rose to their feet and, one by one, approached and touched their master's feet. When it was Govinda's turn to perform this act of submission, Jayananda waited until his student's head was close to his own and then spoke to him in a soft and reassuring voice. "Stay behind," he said.

The last of the disciples completed the ritual and left the meditation grove. Govinda found himself standing alone with Jayananda. "Come with me, Govinda," the tirthankara commanded.

Govinda obediently complied and followed Jayananda towards the river. The place towards which they were headed was the same house where prior to his initiation Govinda had fallen unconscious. Although he often recalled the bliss of those moments, and somewhere deep within secretly longed for their return, since joining the order he had not sought to be alone with Jayananda, nor had the tirthankara required it of him. The warring emotions of desire and anxiety had been enough to keep Govinda aloof. But by the time they had arrived in that very room, and Jayananda had looked at him as only Jayananda could, the rush of adrenalin had again filled Govinda with that repressed sense of exhilaration, and he could feel the promise he had made himself—*not to make Jayananda his new father*—start melting away.

"Wait here, my sweet Govinda." Jayananda's voice was magnetic. "I will return shortly." The tirthankara touched his disciple lightly on the left shoulder and then quietly made his exit into the adjoining room.

Though brief, the contact of Jayananda's hand on his shoulder created a sensation of warmth and well-being within Govinda. Whatever traces of doubt remained seemed to slowly drain from his mind. He walked to the far end of the room and passed through a doorway that opened upon a brightly flowered garden. He stood on the edge of the beds and gazed out at the dancing sea of color. On the horizon he noticed a gathering of billowy dark clouds, and in the near distance he could hear the shrill calls of wandering peacocks.

For some time Govinda stood motionless in the dim sunlight, absorbed in the beauty that surrounded him. Only the eventual sounds of people entering the room behind him broke his aesthetic trance. He turned to see not only Jayananda but also Hriday and Vaikuntha. The latter still had on their orange robes, but Jayananda was dressed in a red and gold sari. His eyebrows and lashes were darkened, and both of his arms were decorated with silver bangles.

Govinda looked at the tirthankara in dismay.

"Come," said Jayananda, beckoning to Govinda with one hand while pointing at a spot on the floor with the other, "sit here."

Govinda did as Jayananda requested and moved almost hypnotically to the center of the room. At the feet of Hriday and Vaikuntha he squatted down.

Jayananda wandered to the far side of the room where he took a seat on a large pillow. He remained completely still with his hands folded together and his eyes closed.

"Look Bandevi," Hriday addressed Vaikuntha. "Who is that sitting alone over there in the forest?" The disciple gestured in the direction of the pillow.

"Don't you know?" Vaikuntha replied. "That is Chandravali, the daughter of the cowherd chief."

"If she is of such high estate, then why ever is she sitting there?" Hriday asked. "Why is she all alone?"

Vaikuntha threw his hands above his head. "God only knows. She often sits there and babbles to herself. Some say she has gone mad over the swami of this forest. Others just say she is insane."

At first Govinda was confused by the speeches of his fellow disciples. Then it dawned on him that he was in fact watching a play in which Jayananda, Hriday, and Vaikuntha were the characters.

"Let's go speak to her," Vaikuntha continued.

Govinda glanced over at Jayananda. He was no longer in his meditative posture. Instead, his head tilted back and his arms and hands stretched out on each side of his body. The palm of his left hand faced forward, while the palm of his right hand turned backward. His eyes, however, remained closed.

"O forest queen," Vaikuntha said as the two disciples arrived at Jayananda's side. "Why are you sitting here in such a state of anticipation? Do you know something we don't know, or see something we don't see?"

Jayananda did not respond to the question. He simply fluttered the fingers of both hands and rocked slightly forward.

"She is not in her proper senses," Hriday said. "She does not even know what you are asking her?"

"Don't your hear me, Chandravali?" This time Vaikuntha's voice was raised to the level of a shout.

Jayananda maintained his upward gaze. "Yes, I hear you, but why do you shout? You will scare him away."

"Who?" said Hriday

"The thief, of course." Jayananda answered.

"Which thief?"

"The thief of my heart. Don't you see, I have trapped him in my eyes, so if you cry out and I open them, he will escape."

Vaikuntha gently placed his hand on the upper part of Jayananda's back, and Jayananda responded by energetically jumping to his feet and firmly grabbing onto the disciple's arm.

"Oh speak to me, my beloved thief," he said in a raised and shrill voice.

Vaikuntha removed his arm from Jayananda's grasp.

"Where will you flee now?" Jayananda snapped.

Together the two disciples hurriedly walked some distance from the pillow, leaving the tirthankara to lament alone.

Jayananda opened his eyes. "Just look at that treacherous one," he cried. "He refused my hand, and then shamefully and without concern he fled from me once again. Who knows where he has gone now?"

The final word had not yet left his mouth when Jayananda started moving madly about, scurrying first in one direction and then another. "Where are you hiding, you cheat?" he called each time he took up a new course.

What struck Govinda as he watched the unfolding scene was just how earnest Jayananda was in his dramatic display. Whereas both Hriday and Vaikuntha acted in a manner befitting a performance, Jayananda's delivery was much more engaging. He seemed to have actually become Chandravali.

Jayananda returned to the pillow. "Please speak to me!" he shouted. "Speak to me! . . .Then remain silent. I will find you myself."

Again he began dashing to and fro. This time he accompanied his scramble with song. "Tell me dear trees, have you seen my beloved? Now that he has left me, where has he gone? Tell me O grove, O forest, O vine, did you see that charming boy? O river, O birds, O butterflies, have you not seen the love of my life?"

Hriday's sharp whistle brought Jayananda's wanderings to a halt.

"Aha, my beloved calls to me," the tirthankara exclaimed. "I must be ready for him." He straightened the sari and rearranged his bangles.

Vaikuntha reappeared and cautiously took the tirthankara by the hand. "And where is it that you are going, my dear Chandravali?" he asked.

Jayananda looked at the disciple as if his question were some kind of trick. "To meet him, of course," he ultimately replied.

Hriday now joined Vaikuntha. "My dear girl," he said to Jayananda. "Do you know where you are and what time it is?"

Jayananda fidgeted with his bangles and said nothing.

Hriday provided the answer. "You are in the middle of the forest, and it is near midnight. Don't you care what people will say?"

Hriday's words seemed to rekindle a distant memory. Jayananda stopped his fidgeting and closed his eyes. "Oh yes, now I remember," he whispered. "I am in the forest, lost in that treacherous forest created purely for his own sport."

There was an extended period of silence, and Govinda ventured that one of the three might have forgotten his lines, but then Jayananda audaciously bounded to one side of the makeshift stage and covered his head with his hands.

"Oh, but if it was destined to turn out this way, why did that thief speak to me in such alluring images?" The tirthankara's words had yet again taken the form of a loud and anguished cry. "I am a fool, a real fool. I should have known it would eventually come to this. Fate is against me. This is intolerable. He has abandoned me."

Jayananda began to sob. Govinda could see that tears were starting to stream down his face, leaving behind them blurry black traces.

"When I am in such pain why should I care what people think," he lamented. "What are the opinions of others to me when compared to this agony?"

Hriday reached over, took a corner of the sari, and methodically wiped the tears from Jayananda's eyes. "Do not grieve, Chandravali," he said. "Your devotion cannot go unnoticed. We have never seen such a display. Everyone loves, but you are special."

Hriday let the cloth drop and brought his hands reverently to his forehead.

"Forgive me, my companions," Jayananda exclaimed. "I have been so enraptured that I have forgotten to treat you in the fashion that guests deserve."

"Do not speak in such a manner, sweet Chandravali," Vaikuntha hastily responded. "You are more beloved to us than life itself. Just to be near you and see your passionate devotion is more than we deserve."

Jayananda appeared to pay no attention to Vaikuntha's reply. His eyes were suddenly wide open. He raised his left hand to his ear and cocked his head slightly to one side. "Do you hear that?"

"What?" the disciples said in unison.

"That noise, . . . it must be . . ."

"I see nothing," said Hriday.

"No one is there," Vaikuntha confirmed.

"Look, sitting over there in the thicket." Jayananda swiveled his hips and pointed his left forefinger in Govinda's direction. "Look at his beautiful silk garments, whose majestic splendor exceeds even that of the glorious sun. See his charming face and magical moonbeam eyes that drive all the women mad."

"Yes, now I see him," Hriday shouted.

"He is like a lotus amongst the weeds" Vaikuntha chimed in.

Govinda realized what was happening. He felt a sudden constriction in his upper throat. He leaned forward and swallowed hard, but the lump would not leave him. He was not looking directly at the tirthankara, but he could still feel the penetrating power of Jayananda's frenzied stare.

Jayananda pointed back at Govinda. "Quickly, friends," he shouted, "capture the clever thief before he runs away."

In an instant Hriday and Vaikuntha were at Govinda's side. They helped him to stand and escorted him towards the pillow that now lay at Jayananda's feet.

The prisoner followed the two men's hand-given instructions and seated himself on the soft, rectangular surface. No sooner had Govinda become still than Jayananda began to slowly circumambulate the pillow. The guru's eyes remained fixed on his captured disciple. He shuffled his feet from side to side. His hips swayed rhythmically, and his hands formed themselves into numerous stylized gestures.

Govinda hypnotically followed Jayananda's path. He turned his head as far as his neck would stretch until finally the tirthankara passed out of sight. With Jayananda temporarily behind him, Govinda fleetingly glanced over at Hriday and Vaikuntha. Both seemed completely absorbed in their master's dance. He wanted to turn around, but some internal force prevented him from doing so. He could feel his heart beating ever faster.

Jayananda was now singing. The beat of his song matched the dynamic flow of his hands and feet. "Now that you are finally here, O precious one, O thief of my heart, I beg you not to leave. Do not abandon me for other delights. My desire for your presence will burn itself into nothingness."

Jayananda repeated these verses several times. He was again standing directly in front of Govinda.

The singing stopped, and the pace of his movement gradually quickened. His feet shuffled ever more rapidly, and his body dipped and swayed with greater regularity. When he was behind Govinda for the second time, the tirthankara's entire torso began to shake, and as he came back into view his writhing reached fever pitch. His ankles moved with staccato-like speed. His bangles clanged noisily together. His neck constantly jutted in and out, and his shoulders heaved heavily back and forth. He continued this way for another complete revolution, and then in one climactic gesture he tossed himself to the ground, placed his head on the edge of the pillow near Govinda's feet, and let out a long, painful groan.

Jayananda lay frozen where he had fallen. Govinda was still too overcome with the spectacle to say anything, and both Hriday and Vaikuntha seemed lost in their gazes of admiration.

Eventually the tirthankara began to stir. Soon he was again on his feet. Govinda carefully examined his countenance and instantly noticed that his disposition had changed. A certain aloofness seemed to have come over him. He slowly and steadily backed away from the pillow. "I must go home now," he declared. "Ma will wonder where I have been."

The disciples also departed. Govinda was left alone to fathom what he had just seen.

Chapter 21

Y ou should feel honored," Hriday attested. "Shri Jayananda has brought you into his special circle. Very few are invited there."

"That may be," Govinda acknowledged, "but it all seems so strange. It is a completely different world, and, to be honest, I am not sure I am suited for such a world."

The two disciples stood together at the far western edge of the large orchard that separated the temple's back gate from its main water tank. It was late in the afternoon, and the shadows of the numerous fruit trees had grown long. A warm breeze tickled the foliage.

Hriday picked a blossom from a nearby tree and twirled it between his fingers. "Yes, it is certainly a very different world," he said. "It is a world of pure devotion."

"But sometimes it all seems so childish, with all of the dancing and singing and dressing up and . . ." Govinda was just about to be completely candid but at the last moment thought better of it.

Hriday ignored the break in Govinda's comment. "Again you are correct." He dropped the blossom on the ground and pushed it with his toes. "Yes, it is childish, but it is this very childishness that leads one to the most profound truths."

"I have trouble grasping those truths, my brother," Govinda responded. "It is rather when I hear Shri Jayananda preach the path of the Vedanta and behold his superior powers of detachment and self control that I sense the truth, for it is then that I feel a sense of my own inner powers. When I watch him playing these games, my soul is . . . "

"Excited?" Hriday cautiously filled in the blank.

The young disciple did not reply.

"Let me speak candidly, Govinda. I have observed you closely on these occasions, and although you may say that you find them awkward, and I do believe you, there is also little doubt in my mind that at such times your soul is stirred."

Govinda reached out and plucked a withering blossom. "I will not disagree with you that the experiences are exhilarating," he concurred at last, "but they are matters of the heart."

"Yes. And that is exactly the insight Shri Jayananda is attempting to demonstrate - that the most profound truths reside in the heart, not in the head, not even in the deepest realms of the psyche."

Hriday's argument contained no logical contradiction, and yet it seemed to Govinda that it went against the spirit of the tirthankara's teachings on the Vedanta. "But it is also true that the heart can be deceptive," he asserted. "Has not Shri Jayananda himself taught us that the primary source of our various afflictions is ignorance, and that the source of our ignorance is taking what is non-eternal to be the eternal? And does not the heart do exactly that: grasp at the non-eternal?"

"That depends."

"On what?"

"On the nature of one's soul."

Govinda angled his head. "Please explain," he said.

"I once heard Shri Jayananda clarify this truth as follows: In this world there exist those souls who are, what we might call, 'regular' or 'normal' souls, and in the case of such souls your observation certainly applies. These souls are found among the masses of people who are attached to the objects of this world. They use the word 'love' as a symbol of that attachment. In their hearts, they do not long for that which is eternal. Rather, they desperately cling to desire, and thus the only path that will lead them to liberation is the path that requires giving up love altogether."

Hriday stopped his explanation to see if Govinda wanted to comment. The ensuing silence gave him his answer.

"But for those special souls, those who are on a higher plane and are well-nourished in the true knowledge of themselves and the world, love becomes the highest expression of their liberation. Their love is no longer directed towards the objects of this world but towards the divine."

This time Govinda did not remain quiet. "If that is so, then why does Shri Jayananda spend so much time extolling the virtues of the Vedantic path which holds as its anchor the extinction of self?" There was a plea in his question.

Hriday took a deep breath. "Please do not misunderstand me," he said. "The way of Vedanta is a very sacred path, and it is not to be taken lightly. But there are different levels of understanding. The highest form of self-extinction is devotion, and thus only devotion can take the soul to the highest levels of realization."

Hriday lightly closed his eyes and searched his memory. "As Shri Jayananda once recounted: 'That which is the greatest state is divine love, the emergence of which destroys the darkening ignorance of all other forms of knowledge. Such love is the path which leads to the extinction of the self. Indeed it is the true extinction of self.'"

Govinda looked up into the cloudless sky. "But if I understand you correctly," he said, "not all of us are capable of attaining this state?"

"This is so, Govinda. Just as all people are not capable of attaining the deeper knowledge of the Vedanta, and therefore live their lives on the level of life we call convention, so not all higher souls are qualified for this special knowledge. And that is precisely why Shri Jayananda has created his inner circle. These are the souls which he has identified as having the ability to manifest divine love."

"Well, then, perhaps Shri Jayananda has made a mistake with me." Govinda peeked at Hriday so see his reaction.

The older disciple shook his head vigorously. "A tirthankara does not make such mistakes," he protested. " Of one thing you can be sure Govinda, Shri Jayananda would not have brought you into the inner circle if he were not certain of your spiritual capacities."

Govinda turned inward. He questioned whether he should continue the conversation and reveal to the disciple the depth of his own inner turmoil?

"But my feelings are torn . . ." the words seemed to jump uncontrollably out of Govinda's mouth. "It is as if I am being violently pulled in two different directions, and I am afraid that I might come apart."

"You must be patient, my brother."

Hriday put his arm on Govinda's shoulder. "If it is of any consolation, I can tell you that it took me a long time to finally understand the meaning of true devotion. As you have perceived, the world of Shri Jayananda's inner circle is a very different world, just as the world of childhood is different from the world of adulthood, or the world of the disciple is different from the world of the ordinary man. And as for coming apart, as you call it, think of it as the initial stage of self-extinction . . . Now we should go. The others will be waiting for us in the sanctuary."

"Wait."

"Yes, Govinda."

"Why is it that when he is with the inner circle Shri Jayananda often dresses up like a woman?"

"Why did the great sixteenth century master, Chaitanya, dress like a woman?"

Govinda stood still.

"Because he saw in Krishna's consort, Radha, the supreme manifestation of devotion, and he desired to exemplify her."

Govinda let go of the blossom. "But some say that Chaitanya was not a mere mortal, that he was an avatar, an incarnation of God."

Hriday smiled and nodded his head in assent. "Yes," he said. "Yes."

Chapter 22

It was nearly two hours before their scheduled meeting with Jayananda, but the disciples were hastily making their way towards the meditation hut. News had come to the men via Hriday that the tirthankara urgently wanted to speak to all of them and that there was no time to waste. Govinda speculated that perhaps someone had died, but he kept his thoughts to himself. Next to him he could hear several of the young men openly making their own guesses as to the reason for the change.

They entered the building. It immediately became obvious to everyone that Jayananda was upset. The tirthankara sat in the same lotus position he always assumed when meeting with the complete assemblage of disciples, but on this occasion his face appeared stern and his body tight. A few of his closest followers, notably Hriday and Vaikuntha, were aware of his mental condition and the event that had caused it, but most of the young men, including Govinda, were at loose ends to try and understand the noticeable alteration in their master's demeanor.

The disciples took their usual spots on the floor, and it was not too long before they became aware that a space in the semi-circle was unoccupied. Haladhari, one the youngest and most favored of the new devotees, was missing. Some thought that he might have been detained, but others with greater perception made the association between the young man's absence and Jayananda's manifest displeasure.

In the midst of their ruminations, Jayananda raised his voice. "What is it that stands between the family man and his quest for God? It is not a single obstacle but a double impediment—desire and riches. And together these two encumbrances represent the quintessence of maya, man's attachment to and need for things transient. Together they create the bondage of the spirit."

Jayananda was now shouting. "It is desire and riches that binds a man and deprives him of his essential freedom. For desire, a man becomes a slave, and in allowing for his serfdom, a man loses his freedom."

This was not the first time Govinda had heard Jayananda refer to family life as a type of trap to be avoided, but he had never heard him express his views on the matter with such forcefulness.

The tirthankara did not allow his disciples too much time for reflection, "Everyday you can see the unenviable condition of the new householder. All these young men serving their various masters who kick them daily into occupational submission. And what is the cause of this occupational tyranny? Desire. When you marry, you settle down in the marketplace. All of your actions are now directed to the values of this market place. Thus does the marketplace become your bondage. And why are you in such bondage? The pull of riches, which is inseparable from desire."

Jayananda glared towards the back of the room. The disciples stole apprehensive glances at one another.

"Just look and see the bewitching power young women have over men." Jayananda's commanding voice once more filled the air. "These women with their sweet perfumes, braided hair, and darkened eyes are the embodiment of the world's delusion. They trick men. They make them into cowardly crawling creatures. When I see a man sitting with a young woman I say to myself, "He is done for; he is lost . . . Haladhari was such a nice boy, but now a witch possesses him. Most of you are probably asking, where is Haladhari? Where do you expect him to be? Copulating with his witch bride!"

There was a brief stirring as the disciples now realized what had happened.

"So you see, my beloved ones," Jayananda was again preaching, "you should be sure to keep far away from such females. Only then will you be able to gain self-realization. It is very harmful to a man's soul to have anything to do with women who have bad motives. They rob a man of his true being. As the old proverb says: 'Woman devours the three worlds.' When such women see handsome young men, they lay traps for them. Marriage and the life of the householder is the trap they lay down."

Jayananda seemed to have finished his tirade. He took a deep breath and closed his eyes. The disciples understood his actions to indicate he was preparing himself for meditation. But just as a sense of calm was coming over the group, Jayananda punctured the quiet.

"The female body is the symbol of the prison of worldly interests," he proclaimed at the top of his voice. "What is there in that body? Nothing but blood, flesh, fat, pus, urine, and feces. And to these things men are attracted? Why? Why are men attracted to dirt and filth? Like small children, they are attracted to a few moments of transient pleasure. Woman is like a mother who peels their bananas for them."

Jayananda's last statement brought a few faint smiles to the faces of several of the followers, but the tirthankara's stern brow quickly removed their smirks. Then from the far end of the circle a hand was timidly raised. Jayananda noticed it and nodded his permission for the disciple to speak.

"Forgive me, Shri Jayananda," the boy said in a faint voice, "but if what you say is true, then our mothers and fathers are part of the trap."

Govinda admired the young disciple's courage. A similar thought had passed through his own mind, but given Jayananda's disposition he had not even considered raising it. Now he looked carefully at the tirthankara to see his reaction.

Jayananda's countenance remained austere. "Your question must be approached on two different levels. First, there is the level of the ordinary, unenlightened soul. Such souls are not capable of attaining complete self-realization in this life. Their role is that of the householder, and more than that cannot be expected from them. Yet, even on this level, there are those householders who are moderate in their means and desires and those who become obsessed with the possessions of the world. For souls of this nature, there is no real harm in gaining wealth, as long as that wealth does not become an end unto itself but rather is seen as a source for serving what is good . . .

The same can be said regarding a householder's relationship with his wife. A householder may share his bed with the woman and bring several children into the world, but on no account should he allow himself to become emotionally attached, either to her or his children. In his heart, there should only be compassion. The household should be viewed as a foreign land where one must work and fulfill one's duties."

Jayananda stopped to allow the disciples time to digest the first part of the explanation. When he was satisfied that they had grasped his message, he continued.

"But there is another level of soul, the enlightened soul, who is not destined to become a householder. For such a one, householding and all of its snares should be avoided like the plague. It is concerning the enlightened soul that I speak to you today . . .

Should the mothers or fathers of enlightened souls require them to become householders, to become weighed down by the concerns of desire and riches, then, indeed, they are part of the trap. In truth, the enlightened soul has neither earthly mother nor father. His mother is Ma, and his father is Ma. And if the enlightened soul should succumb to that world and be drawn into it, then his soul becomes split. He is forced to pursue ends for which he has not been created. This is why I say a witch has possessed Haladhari. That witch is none other than his lust for the female form, and for that mere sack of pus, bones, and urine, this enlightened one has thrown away his calling. He now aims to please his own desires and those of his wife . . . .

My beloved ones, the role of the enlightened soul is only one: to please Ma and her eternal manifestations."

Govinda noticed that the tirthankara's gaze was aimed directly at him.

Chapter 23

By the next day Jayananda's anger had markedly subsided. It was still apparent to the disciples, however, that the tirthankara was not himself. His morning discourse was dispassionate. On several occasions he seemed to lose his train of thought, and at one point he even stopped altogether and peered dishearteningly away from the eager faces sitting before him. To a man, they thought that the cause of his dejection was Halidhari's betrayal.

Jayananda brought the session to an end, bid his disciples farewell and exited the meditation hut. He needed to get away. Not only were his spirits down, but the hacking cough which had bothered him for the last several weeks had slowly drained him of much of his physical energy. To be in the presence of others, even those in his inner circle, had become a burden. Moreover, despite his almost incessant pleas, during this time of illness Ma Tara had not once spoken to him.

His path took him towards the temple's pine grove whose dozen or so tightly packed trees sat snuggled up against the Ganges and provided a virtual haven from the rest of the compound. This was one of his favorite areas, and he was hoping that its peaceful surroundings would bring him both the solitude and spiritual comfort he so desired. He was somewhat surprised, therefore, that upon entering the sanctuary he spotted Rukhmini sitting in quiet repose at the base of one of the larger trees. He had not seen her for several months. It had been rumored that she had made a pilgrimage to the shrines of Shiva in the Himalayas.

Jayananda was amazed at how happy he was to see the bhairavi. The mood he had carried with him from the meditation hut started to alter. He hurried to the tree, placed his hands on her feet, and sat down. "You have been gone for quite some time," he said. "I was told that you went to the mountains."

Before Rukhmini could answer, Jayananda began coughing. After several loud and raspy hacks, he expelled a large wad of slimy green mucus, which he hastily deposited on the ground next to him.

"You are sick," the woman asserted.

Jayananda tilted his head left then right. "I have been bringing up spittle for a number of days," he confessed.

Rukhmini looked over at the spittle and then back at Jayananda. "When the body is sick, the source of the ailment is generally located in the spirit," she said. "There must be some unfulfilled desire within you."

Jayananda sensed that Rukhmini had grasped his condition. "One of the disciples has left the temple to get married," he responded.

"That is all? There is nothing more?"

"No."

Rukhmini did not delay her reply. "You are not very good at deception, Shri Jayananda," she said. "There is something else."

How does she know these things, Jayananda wondered.

The bhairavi interrupted his thought with more questions. "Could it be that Ma Tara is not speaking to you? Or that Govinda has not displayed his love for you? Or perhaps both?"

Jayananda understood that the bhairavi had read his soul. "I brought Govinda into the inner circle," he disclosed, "and yet for some reason he still remains reticent. He only takes part halfheartedly. He has easily mastered the knowledge of the Vedanta but virtually ignores the other paths."

"Have you told him who he really is?"

"No."

"And why not?"

"I have not seen him display the proper signs that he is prepared for this knowledge. I also sense that such a revelation might well cause him to become frightened and result in his leaving the temple. I remember well how fear blocked my own self-understanding when I was younger. I know its power, and I can see that there is such fear in Govinda's heart."

Jayananda coughed, but did not bring up phlegm.

"Then perhaps you first need to tell him who you really are," Rukhmini asserted.

Jayananda looked perplexed. Rukhmini knew that she must explain. "Let me tell you about my pilgrimage to Kailasa," she said. "I was performing the great circle ritual with the other pilgrims. The path circumventing the mountain is about twenty-five miles in length, and all along the route are scattered shrines, some to the Lord Shiva and others to Parvati, Kali, and Ganesh. After visiting these spots, I asked one older sadhu if he knew where I might find a shrine to Ma Tara, and he took me to a small overgrown canyon several miles off the main path. There in the thick underbrush, almost invisible to the eye, was a deteriorating building. I entered the shrine, cleared away the vines and decaying matter from Ma's image, and sat down . . .

For nearly an hour, I meditated, consumed all the substances, and called upon Ma to make her presence known to me. It started to rain. Another hour passed. I was beginning to think that Ma had abandoned the site when her voice filled my head. She asked me why I had come and what I wanted. I told her that I was concerned about your welfare, that since the coming of Govinda you had not been yourself."

Jayananda coughed and spit out the residue. Rukhmini waited until she once again had his complete attention.

"Then Ma told me that you were not well, that your sickness was due to the fact that the agnivesha would not play the game, and that he would not play the game until he knew exactly who he was and who you were."

This time Jayananda voiced his mounting confusion. "He knows very well who I am. I am his tirthankara."

"After that Ma Tara said no more."

Jayananda pulled slightly back, brought his hand to a spot just above his right eye and looked down to the ground.

The bhairavi reached down into the cloth bag attached to the side of her robe and removed a small object. She stretched out her hand in the direction of Jayananda. "This was at the foot of Ma Tara's image," she said

It was a small, dirt-encrusted icon of two figures whose arms were amorously wrapped around each other. Jayananda closely inspected the statue and recognized the two as Radha and Krishna. He turned the image over in his hand several times while continuing to carefully examine it. Then with a sudden burst of energy he rose dramatically to his feet. "I will not play this game with her any longer!" he announced.

The tirthankara offered no salutation. He clutched the icon tightly in his left hand and scampered across the grove.

Rukhmini knew his destination. "He is coming to you Ma," she whispered. "Jayananda is coming to you."

Jayananda arrived at the sanctuary of the Ma Tara temple. He found several priests busily preparing for the afternoon offerings. "Leave here at once," he yelled. "I need to be alone with Ma."

Initially the pujaris responded with a mild protest, but when they saw the wild look in Jayananda's eyes, they scurried away. "And tell the others not to bother us," the tirthankara shouted behind them.

The sanctuary was empty. Jayananda approached the image. He stood before it and silently observed his beloved deity. For some reason his mind focused on the patches of red that adorned Ma's icon: the four red palms, the red mask surrounding the eyes, and the lolling red tongue.

"Why is it, Ma, that you play with me so?" he asked in an anguished tone. "Have I not served you well? Have I not invited the agnivesha into my family to teach him as you instructed?"

Jayananda waited impatiently for a reply, but the image seemed to stare through him. "Why do you not speak to me?

Tell me why he refuses to surrender his heart to you."

His last question was still ringing in his ears when he began to feel faint. He dropped awkwardly to his knees. He knew he was going into trance. . . .

"Do not fret, Jayananda." Ma Tara's voice penetrated his solitude. "You and the agnivesha cannot manifest the divine game of lila until both you and he know who you are . . . Who are you Jayananda? All the spiritual paths, Vedanta, bhakti, and tantra, have taught you that you and I are one, but there is one more secret they have not taught you, and that is the nature of our oneness."

Jayananda was gradually absorbed into the epiphany. The goddess' face became larger. All he could see was her white eyes and blue visage. Soon it was as if his own face were directly up against hers.

"Listen to me, Jayananda. You are my avatar, my incarnation. I have become you for the sole purpose of my lila. Once the agnivesha hears this, he will recall his own divine station, and there will be no hesitation on his part. Now you must go and reveal yourself to him. Then he must merge into you as you have merged into me."

Ma Tara's voice disappeared, and the contours of her face gradually receded. Jayananda was once again present in the temple sanctuary. He looked up at the goddess. Her palms were still red and turned outward, and her drawn sword and accessories remained the same, but in place of her steel-cold eyes and lolling tongue, he now saw the traces of his own visage. His joy knew no bounds. Compared to what he was now experiencing his past revelations were as cups of water to the entire Ganges. He could only sit and gaze at himself in awe.

Behind him Jayananda could hear the pujaris returning to the sanctuary. He rose to his feet and started to walk in their direction. They stood aside and allowed him to pass. He stepped out into the open courtyard and listened for their gasps of astonishment. He looked down at the image of Radha and Krishna, which he still cradled gently in his hand, and smiled. At the same time he let out four loud coughs and brought into his mouth a large amount of spittle which he instantly ejected on to the ground. On the surface of the large green and yellow mass of mucus were six red patches.

Chapter 24

The day of the annual celebration of Ma Tara puja had arrived. It was mid-morning. The twelve disciples of the inner circle had followed Jayananda's orders of the previous evening and assembled in the meditation hut. Scattered on the floor of the building near its east wall they found numerous items including flowers, incense, sandal-paste, fruits, and assorted sweets.

The main ceremony was not scheduled to occur until later that evening in the inner sanctuary of the Ma Tara Temple. When the disciples observed the paraphernalia they assumed that Jayananda had decided some preparatory worship was necessary. The only question that crossed some of their minds was what image of Ma Tara would be utilized for the morning puja. None of them could ever recall a puja to Ma Tara being celebrated on temple grounds outside of the goddess' sacred abode.

"Shri Jayananda will no doubt bring an image with him," Vaikuntha said

Several of the men nodded their agreement.

The disciples remained alone in the meditation hut, milling about and wondering, both silently and aloud, when the tirthankara would arrive

Jayananda made his appearance. All of the men except Govinda instantaneously hurried towards him in order to touch his feet. The guru hastily motioned them away and proceeded directly to the area where the puja items were located.

He sat down next to the pile of flowers. The disciples assembled themselves on the floor around him. His face was beaming with a broad smile. There was no sign of any image of Ma Tara.

The disciples sat quietly and waited for Jayananda to speak, but much to their surprise, he said nothing. Neither did he make any effort to gather the puja offerings together. After some time Govinda could sense a growing unrest among the young men. Most of them had thought that the tirthankara would orchestrate whatever events were supposed to take place, but instead he continued to just sit and smile. He was not in samadhi; they had observed him many times in that state of deep meditation, and they knew its signs well. No, he was purposefully sitting and waiting, as if he, too, expected something to just miraculously happen.

It was Hriday who finally broke the monotony. He had innately comprehended that his master's continued silence in the presence of the puja offerings could mean only one thing: he wanted his disciples to worship the mother goddess within him by offering puja to his own human image.

Hriday arose and started gathering up various items from the piles of puja offerings. When his arms were full, he approached Jayananda, bowed and meticulously set the offerings at his feet.

The other disciples saw Hriday's act of devotion and quickly followed his example. Soon an overflowing mound of flowers, nuts, sweet meats, and fruit lay in front of their guru. Even Govinda was swept up in the rising emotion of the moment, and when all of the other disciples had finished making their offerings and returned to their respective spots on the floor, he completed the ritual by gently placing several large white lotuses in Jayananda's lap.

Govinda seated himself on the floor amongst the other young men and looked up at Jayananda. The tirthankara's appearance began to dramatically change. His eyes started to dilate, and his hair stood on end. The disciples all recognized that he was now entering samadhi.

Then something unusual took place. Jayananda's body began to methodically twist and gyrate. He managed to contort his limbs into a position that resembled the iconographic form of Ma Tara. To the disciples' complete astonishment, the bottoms of his feet and the palms of his hands were deep red in color.

"And who do you say I am?"

Jayananda's words were unexpected and shocked many of the disciples. Moreover, his voice was much higher in pitch than normal, so much so, that many of them were not even sure it was his.

Hriday did not hesitate to provide an answer. "O Shri Jayananda," he bellowed, "you are none other than the avatar of Ma Tara, an incarnation come to earth out of your mercy for all living beings."

The disciples looked at Jayananda for confirmation. Several of them had their mouths open, and all had stretched the skin around their eyes.

"What more shall I say?" the voice responded. "Gaze upon my right hands, and you shall have all of your desires fulfilled; gaze upon my left hands and you shall never again know fear. These are my boons to all of you."

"Victory to Shri Jayananda," Hriday cried out. "Victory to Ma Tara's avatar."

One by one, the disciples picked up the chant. Soon the entire room resonated with the sounds of their voices.

The men repeated their new-found mantra. Their master swayed his upper body from side to side and began calling them forward by name. In an orderly procession, each young man arose, approached the human icon and then bent down to touch his feet. Jayananda in turn touched their shoulders, first with his hands and then with his feet.

Govinda watched attentively. The very instant a disciple felt Jayananda's touch, he appeared to become the recipient of unlimited ecstasy. Some of the men continued chanting, but in even more exalted tones; others began dancing wildly; still others stayed near the avatar and gazed at him adoringly.

"And my beloved Govinda, . . ." Jayananda had waited

until all of the other disciples had received their blessings before calling upon his favorite.

I am not worthy, Govinda had planned to say, but almost against his will he found himself being propelled toward the avatar by some mysterious inner force. He lay prostrate at Jayananda's feet.

Jayananda's hands made contact with his shoulders. Govinda felt that same exhilarating burst of energy that he had encountered on other occasions when the tirthankara had chosen to touch him. But when Jayananda raised his left foot and let it drop just behind the young man's neck it was as if he had been hit by a thunderbolt. All of the nerves in his body were suddenly pulsating with a constant and explosive excitement. He raised his head and looked around. Everything upon which his eyes focused, be it flower, fruit or man, seemed to be transformed into the self-subsisting center of the universe. The meaning of each and every image appeared to be contained in its very existence.

Govinda gazed intently at whatever objects crossed his line of vision. He could faintly hear Jayananda's soft whisper: "O ancient one, you have been sent to worship and be worshipped by means of the secret door. This is my gift to you sweet agnivesha."

"Secret door . . ." the sounds of the words reverberated throughout Govinda's consciousness. "Secret door," he repeated several times as if he were trying to recall a misplaced memory. Then suddenly he remembered the dream, but this time he did not experience fear, only the joy of complete surrender.

"agnivesha, . . ." his mind switched gears . . . "agnivesha . . ."

At first there was only a hazy intimation, but ever-so-slowly the veil of forgetfulness started to lift. His present identity with its ingrained psychic construction began to crumble. He felt himself being drawn back to some long-lost, forgotten place and time where Govinda neither existed nor did not exist but merely appeared to be an apparition among many other such apparitions.

The young man looked up at Jayananda. The tirthankara's

serene eyes were like mirrors in which he could see a myriad of images—prince, pauper, honey, feces, saint, prostitute—they were all there, side by side, with countless others. His eyes became watery. He reached up and stroked Jayananda's foot. "O Ma," he softly muttered. Jayananda in turn reached down and affectionately caressed the back of Govinda's neck.

Jayananda allowed the disciples to remain in their blissful states for much of the afternoon. He further intoxicated them with both song and dance so that their ecstasy knew no limits. Then, as the sun began its descent over the Ganges, he brought them back to the mundane world of the meditation hut, the temple grounds, and their own insubstantial selves. He repositioned himself in the lotus position. With the sound of his normal voice the world of lila disappeared.

"It is time to prepare for the evening's celebrations."

The startled disciples all felt as if they had been violently awakened from a deep sleep. Many shook their heads uncontrollably, and two or three cried out that they did not want the rapture to end.

"You have tasted the honey," Jayananda said. "The honey will not lose its sweetness because you have to shit."

A gush of laughter broke the tension.

"Now listen very closely my children . . . What you have learned, and what you have seen here today is for the moment part of the secret doctrine. A time will soon come when this knowledge will be made manifest to all, but for now it is to remain only with you. Do you understand?"

All the disciples assented.

"Then go take care of your needs before the throngs arrive."

The disciples stood up and prepared to touch the avatar's feet. As he had done earlier, Jayananda motioned them away. "It is not necessary," he said "Save your devotion for this evening."

The room began to clear.

"Govinda!" Jayananda interjected as the last of the men slowly approached the door. "You can stay."

Hriday heard the command and remained close to

Jayananda. The senior disciple hoped that he too would be invited to stay, but when the room was finally empty the newly proclaimed avatar calmly dashed his hopes. "We need to be alone," he said in a matter-of-fact manner.

Hriday bowed his consent and turned to leave.

Govinda looked at Jayananda apprehensively.

"There is one more secret I need to teach you."

As he was passing through the door Hriday heard the word 'secret.' When he was outside he immediately found Vaikuntha who could see by the disconcerted look on his companion's face that all was not well. "What is the matter, Hriday?" he asked.

"Why is it that Govinda gets such special attention? - especially when it is evident to everyone that among all of the members of the inner circle he is the least devoted."

Vaikuntha did not answer.

Chapter 25

Govinda was strolling peacefully through the temple's sprawling flower garden, lost in the beauty of the moment and feeling the divine presence all around him. In the distance he spied a tall, dark-complexioned man whom he recognized as Manindra's personal attendant. The servant was coming rapidly towards him, and his gait had a look of urgency about it. Govinda wondered if something might be wrong.

"Manindra Babu needs to see you," the servant called as he came within speaking distance. "He is waiting in his office."

"I must first perform my morning ablutions," Govinda responded. "Tell Manindra Babu that I will come shortly."

The servant stopped, remained stationary and pursed his lips.

"I will be there soon," Govinda repeated.

The man seemed to finally understand and left as quickly has he had come.

Govinda knew that mundane thoughts would taint the potency of his ablutions. Nevertheless, during the entire time that he was crouched down on the bathing ghat's lowest step, covering his head and shoulders with ritualistic pourings of water from the Ganges, he could not take his mind off the servant's poignant message. *Whatever could the temple owner want?* Since he had joined the community Manindra had only spoken to him once, on the day he had taken his vows, and then only in the manner of a formal congratulations. *Had he done something wrong? Should he first go tell Shri Jayananda?* Govinda released another handful of water atop his head.

Manindra was also somewhat apprehensive about the appointment, and Govinda's subsequent approach to the house found the temple owner pacing back and forth on the freshly scrubbed tiles of his bedroom balcony, silently rehearsing what he planned to say to his visitor.

The same servant whom he had encountered in the garden met Govinda at the door. The disciple was shown into the parlor where he was left to wait alone for Manindra's descent. As was his custom, Manindra allowed his visitor to linger several minutes before making his own appearance. Ultimately he emerged from the bottom of the staircase. An extensive smile did its best to hide his own wariness.

"Govinda," he boomed in an overly friendly voice. "It is always a pleasure to see one of our prized devotees."

Govinda was not prepared to become engaged in any small talk. He looked directly at the owner and went right to the heart of the matter. "And what exactly is it, Manindra Babu, that we need to discuss?"

The straightforward question appeared to catch Manindra off guard. "Would you like some tea?" he said in response.

"I have had my morning meal."

Manindra rubbed his hands together and walked mechanically towards the massive bookcase that dominated the far wall. When he was within arm's reach of the shelves, he stopped, brought his hands to his chin, and turned around. "I am afraid I have some bad news."

"Could he know?" Govinda wondered.

"You have probably noticed that for some time now Shri Jayananda has been bothered by fairly severe bouts of coughing." The older man's uneven stream of words interrupted Govinda's thoughts.

"At first we assumed that it was merely a case of gathering

phlegm, which, as you certainly know, is not all that uncommon in Benares at this time of year, but when he started to spit up large amounts of blood, I finally convinced him that he should see a Western physician for an opinion."

Manindra halted his explanation and took a deep breath. Govinda tried to prepare himself for what he sensed was coming.

"Dr. Suresh is one of the top medical doctors in all of India. His specialty is the study of cancerous tumors. He has recently informed us that Shri Jayananda has a malignant growth in his chest, . . . and there is fear that the disease may have spread to the lung."

It took some time for these words to register with Govinda. Then it suddenly dawned on him that Jayananda had contracted a fatal disease. "Surely it can be cured," he said. His voice trembled.

Manindra steadied himself. "I am afraid that the cancer is in an advanced stage. Dr. Suresh claims that it is a miracle Shri Jayananda has been able to maintain so much of his strength for such an extended period of time."

Govinda took several steps in Manindra's direction. "But why has Shri Jayananda not told us?" he queried.

"He did not want to cause you concern. And confidentially, he does not know that I am telling you now, and I only do so . . ." Manindra stopped.

Govinda waited.

"Please have a seat." Manindra pointed to a large divan that bisected the room's sprawling blue and beige Persian carpet.

Govinda dutifully followed the temple owner across the floor and sat down on one of the bulging brown cushions.

Manindra waited for the disciple to become comfortable.

"Now listen carefully, Govinda," the man began. "The truth of the matter is that our beloved Shri Jayananda does not have much time to live. I know that this must come as a tremendous shock to you . . . as it did to me . . . and like you, I am deeply and profoundly saddened by the news, but there is one thing you need to understand. We cannot allow this fact of life

to so devastate us that we forget about the significance of our
glorious movement . . . And that is the reason why I have asked
you to come here today. For although Shri Jayananda will die,
we must make it our sacred duty to ensure that we formulate
plans for the movement to successfully live on. Too much time
and energy has been given to this great and holy enterprise to
allow it to collapse because of the death of one man, even if he
is a tirthankara."

Govinda was still trying to come to terms with the fact
that Jayananda would soon depart this world and was not sure
he really understood exactly what Manindra was talking about.
"What do you mean?" he asked.

The owner's answer was blunt and to the point. "I mean
precisely that it is incumbent upon us to find a new leader who
will be able to successfully guide the movement after Shri
Jayananda has left us."

Govinda did not feel like talking about such matters, but
he also knew that he had to respond. "The choice is an obvious one," he eventually replied. "Who among the disciples
knows Shri Jayananda's teachings more clearly or has been
closer to him during the last several years than Hriday?"

Manindra cleared his throat and shook his head from side
to side. "I cannot agree with you," he said in what was little
more than a loud whisper. "Hriday is certainly a good disciple,
and, as you say, he has been close to Shri Jayananda for quite
some time, but this, in fact, is his weakness."

Govinda leaned slightly forward and raised his head. *Who
other than Hriday would be qualified for such a role?*

The owner looked away from the disciple and mulled over
what he would say next. "I am not quite sure how to explain
this," he frankly admitted, "but I think you know that while
Shri Jayananda is a great tirthankara, many of his doctrines are
not easy to understand. At times he appears to live in a world
that seems quite far removed from the knowledge that was
taught by our great Vedantic sages such as Shri
Shankaracharya."

Now that he had established his train of thought
Manindra looked back at his visitor with greater confidence.

"And I think it is fair to say that many of his own disciples are perplexed by his teachings. In fact, were it not for the charismatic power of his personality, I am convinced that many of the movement's most ardent supporters would have long ago abandoned it."

Govinda was dismayed by this revelation, but said nothing.

"When Shri Jayananda is gone we will need someone who can return us to the path of ancient glory, someone who has mastered the manly rigors of self denial, someone who can turn to the poor and dispossessed with compassion, and this is not Hriday. He is too close to Shri Jayananda. He is completely absorbed in the devotion of the feminine. He has forgotten that even Ma Tara worships Shiva."

Govinda put his hands on his knees and cocked his head slightly to one side. "Are you saying that Shri Jayananda's path is not acceptable?"

Manindra moved closer to the young man. "I would not disagree that for a select group of disciples Shri Jayananda's path may indeed be the correct one," he said. "But these teachings are not what India requires at this moment in her history. These are momentous times. We must present ourselves to the world from a position of spiritual strength, and in order to do that we need a path that speaks to the heart and soul of our nation, not just to the mystical tendencies of an elite few."

Certain elements of Manindra's address struck a chord within Govinda. However, a growing irritation with the owner's insensitivity had begun to gnaw at his patience. He silently weighed the pros and cons of expressing his feelings and decided to be forthright.

"Excuse me if I sound rude, Manindra Babu, but I do not see how you can speak about such matters at a time like this. Shri Jayananda may be dying, but for now he is still with us, and I for one want to spend whatever time he has left in this world at his side. To criticize him in this way, at this time, does not seem appropriate."

Manindra stepped back and brought his hands together. "I can understand and appreciate your feelings," he replied, "and for the moment I will say no more. But the fact of the matter is that the movement is greater than any one individual, and it is my responsibility to make sure that it fulfills its destiny . . . That destiny requires solid leadership, and I think you know who must take on the mantle of that leadership."

Govinda stared at Manindra.

"Yes, it is you, Govinda. You must be the next tirthankara."

Chapter 26

Several days after Govinda had been summoned to the private meeting with Manindra, Jayananda spontaneously decided that he wanted to take his inner circle of disciples away from the compound for an afternoon outing. The site he chose for the excursion was one of his favorites. It was located on the northern bank of the Ganges about fifteen miles to the northeast of the temple. The large parcel of sprawling land was owned by one of the temple's most wealthy and avid supporters. Its spacious acreage sported two large dwellings as well as a stable area for horses and other animals. Its gardens were well known throughout the region for both their design and beauty.

Jayananda liked to refer to the location as his "little Brindavan," since its rolling meadows and slow-running, gurgling streams reminded him of that enchanted mythical landscape depicted in one of his favorite texts, the *Bhagavata Purana*, where the young Krishna joyfully dallied with the sons and daughters of the local cowherds.

Whereas on most occasions of this nature the disciples made the journey on foot, on this day Jayananda had ordered several horse-drawn carriages to convey himself and his companions. The tirthankara's face looked obviously drawn, and his body appeared much thinner than usual, but the disciples could sense the presence of an overabundance of playful energy filling their master's being. They all instantly understood that the requisition of the carriages was not so much a result of his ill health as it was an indication that he intended to treat this outing in the manner of one of those special days he referred to as 'Ma's delight.'

The morning was sublime. The thin, filmy layer of dust and haze that normally enshrouded both the city and its surrounding countryside was nowhere to be seen. In its place an almost endless stretch of deep blue sky dominated the heavens, blemished only by an occasional wispy puff of white cloud. There seemed to be a special lightness in the air, while in the various nooks and crannies of the earth below, a pulsating rhythm of primordial vitality was omnipresent. Only the most cynical or world-weary of souls would not be capable of feeling the magical presence of the moment.

After a somewhat lengthy and bumpy trip the three carriages gradually slowed and came to a stop at the side of a narrow dirt road. From their vantage points within the carriages, the disciples could see that they were separated from the fence which formed the perimeter of the property by a small stretch of uncared for soil and brush.

In the near distance there stood a majestic, two-story wooden house whose immaculate ivory-white walls were surrounded by four large banyan trees that protectively canopied several meticulously manicured gardens. From the edge of the roadway to the gardens' first hedges, lush fields of uncut grass and wildflowers swayed this way and that to the whim of the ever-shifting afternoon breeze.

Jayananda was the first to exit the carriage. With seemingly boundless energy, he virtually leapt from its interior, quickly crossed the small stretch of shrub, and then maintained his rapid pace through the shimmering grass. The disciples had to practically run to keep up with him, and by the time the last of them reached the shaded garden area, most were out of breath.

The young men stood quietly under the cooling shade of the massive banyan trees. Jayananda arrived at the house's large veranda, dallied for a moment or two, and then disappeared through a large wooden door. Soon thereafter he reappeared on the porch shadowed by a number of men in costume whom the disciples recognized to be members of a local theatrical troupe. The actors followed Jayananda down the steps and into the garden where they quickly began to situate themselves for what appeared to be the beginning of a performance. Some of the men had musical instruments in their hands, and several others carried large caricature-style masks.

A few actors scurried about making final preparations. Jayananda meanwhile directed the disciples to seat themselves in a semi-circle.

When the players were all in their starting places and Jayananda had joined his disciples on the ground, a hushed quiet fell over the scene.

Two of the actors stepped forward, put their wooden flutes to their mouths and proceeded to fill the air with soft and fluid tones. Another two men moved up next to them and began to sing: "Tell us a story that will gladden our hearts. Recount to us a tale from that most renowned spot on earth called Mathura, and the blessings granted to it by the gods. Give to us an account of a great king and of an even greater one whose very existence brings the world the greatest of joys."

The musicians shuffled backwards, and a man with a large, jewel-studded crown and long-flowing grey beard moved to the front of the assemblage. Another actor who carried on his shoulder a mock weapon accompanied the royal character. "Hail to thee, our most great and noble king, Ugrasen," the man with the weapon sang. "Hail O great protector of cow and brahman."

"Lord Chamberlain," the solemn-looking king replied. "Something has been nagging at my heart recently. As you know, I am well blessed. I have many children and a prosperous kingdom, but of late, I have been feeling strangely guilty that I have not been thankful enough. After a great deal of meditation and reflection, I have decided that I would now like to repent my thoughtlessness and make a luxuriant ceremonial sacrifice to our great Lord of Creation, the eternal and mighty Vishnu."

The lord chamberlain made a deep and overly dramatic

bow. "What a wonderful idea, my lord," he said.

"I am exceedingly glad you agree with me," the king responded. "Then go tell the brahmans to prepare a magnificent altar on the banks of the river Jumana, and make sure that you spare no expense."

Again the lord chamberlain bowed and then awkwardly rambled towards another small group of actors who were standing some distance from center stage. "Your great and most humble monarch, king Ugrasen, has just issued special orders that you, the most holy and learned of his brahmans, prepare a great sacrifice to our Lord Vishnu on the banks of the Jumana," he shouted as he approached them. "Now he needs to know if this request is made at an auspicious time?"

"Well, why not?" the brahmans sang out in unison. "When is the time not auspicious to make sacrifices to the gods?"

Another actor, whose piercing ebony eyes were encircled by dark, shadowy rings, stepped forward. His hair was heavily oiled. His chin and cheeks were covered by a thick, black beard. Above his lip was a curly charcoal mustache.

"And tell me O silly chamberlain, why is it that you always give my naive father such terrible advice," he bellowed. "All these useless and brainless brahmans know how to do is throw meaningless objects into the fire and in the process drain my father's kingdom of its wealth."

The last of these condemnatory remarks had scarcely departed the actor's huge mouth when from his seat on the ground Jayananda impulsively let out a loud and disparaging series of hoots. In response to this unforeseen gesture, the actor jokingly stuck out his large red tongue in the direction of Jayananda and contemptuously wiggled it up and down. This in turn caused an immediate uproar of hilarity among the disciples who were now well aware that the repulsive character upon whom they were focusing their attention was none other than Krishna's mortal and evil enemy, the prince Kans.

"Guards, guards!" Kans yelled, pointing frantically at the priests and at the same time silencing the laughter of the disciples. "Throw these no-good parasites into the Jumana, and make sure that all of their sacrifice-making paraphernalia goes into the water with them. When you are finished with these so-called holy men, take this good-for-nothing lord chamberlain and put him in prison. I will have to council my father before the entire kingdom is made to go bankrupt."

Kans' speech evoked a series of low murmuring and hissing sounds from the disciples. Meanwhile, two new performers armed with spears and swords appeared on the makeshift stage and violently seized the frightened brahmans and cowering lord chamberlain. The prince followed their actions by walking determinedly in the direction of king Ugrasen. His face was etched with a wicked, melodramatic smile.

For the next half hour the play proceeded as both actors and audience knew that it would: Kans quarreled violently with his noble father and, in a fit of rage, eventually slew him. On becoming king, Kans brashly exhibited his gallery of evil qualities: lust, greed, envy, and suspicion. In order to secure his hold on the kingdom, Kans arranged for the immediate marriage of his daughter, Devaki, to an upstanding neighboring dignitary, Vasudeva. When Kans was eventually told by one of his advisors about a certain prophecy that Devaki's eighth-born child would grow up to kill him, the new king responded by setting plans to murder his own daughter. Later he was convinced by Vasudeva to let Devaki live under house arrest until the birth of the baby.

During the unfolding events many of the disciples had started to display their emotions, either by making contorted facial expressions or, in several cases, by vocalizing actual groans of anguish.

Jayananda appeared virtually hypnotized by the drama, and when the story soon shifted to the scene where the devout and loyal Devaki lay despairingly alone in her prison cell, noticeably pregnant with her eighth child, the tirthankara seemed to be on the verge of falling into samadhi. All of the signs were present: the wide-open and dilated eyes, the stiff neck and back, and the undulating body hair.

Suddenly the actor playing Devaki dropped heavily to his knees. In a voice that manifested severe anguish, he pitifully called out to heaven in an attempt to enlist a reaction from the gods. At first he cried to Indra, and when there was no answer, he next directed his petition to lord Shiva. In response a thunderous voice coming from behind the actors directed Devaki to petition Vishnu.

The frantic young woman quickly followed the divine advice. "O Lord of creation," she sobbed, "how can it be that such sin and wickedness can prevail in your world? Why is it that you allow such unrighteousness to triumph while goodness is ground into the dust?"

From the far side of a nearby hedge several of the performers swiftly raised aloft a sizable cardboard representation of Vishnu. The blue-skinned god was pictured reclining on the back of the great serpent, Shesha. All four of his hands were filled with different weapons, and around his neck hung a garland of jeweled flowers. Near Shesha's flanks, and amidst several immense swirling grey and yellow lines, were countless white lotuses with pink centers. The design was undoubtedly meant to remind the viewers of the story they had often heard since childhood concerning the mysterious emergence of all life from a great primeval ocean.

An anonymous, bellowing voice pierced the silence. Even though the disciples knew the words almost by heart, they all remained transfixed. "Do not worry my dear child," the voice said. "All of the terror you have endured is in the cause of ultimate good. Know that our child will be divinely protected, and that he will grow up to be a savior to mankind."

The picture of Vishnu was taken down. The disciples next expected to see the character of Vasudeva return to the stage, fording the Jumana river with the image of Krishna on his shoulders, since this was the traditional means used by most theatrical groups to symbolize the divinely guided evacuation of the child-god to the countryside for safe keeping from Kans. But just as the actors began to reassemble in front of the hedge, Jayananda leapt to his feet, grabbed Govinda by the hand, and rushed among them.

The devotees could hardly believe their eyes. The tirthankara lifted Govinda up upon his shoulders and carried him across the strip of blue carpet that had been rolled out in front of the foliage. The master then gently lowered his disciple to the ground, immediately dropped to his knees, and ceremoniously touched the young man's feet.

Everyone knew that the symbolic gesture could only have one meaning.

Chapter 27

Jayananda was dead.

It seemed to his disciples that for months his mighty spirit had drawn on an almost boundless source of energy, but the malignancy that was slowly consuming his frail body could not be stopped. The day came when the avatar could no longer move freely around the temple grounds, and it was not too long afterwards that he was confined to his house. In the end he was forced to take permanently to his bed.

In the manner of a loyal son, Govinda was at his master's side almost day and night, softly massaging his legs and feet with his hands and soothing his soul with his tender words. Chandramani was also present, but it was readily apparent whose company the dying man preferred.

When he could no longer speak, the avatar took to writing down his messages on small scraps of paper. As far as anyone could remember, outside of a few personal letters and official documents, these were the only words their guru had written since the day he had abandoned the classroom. The notes were generally short and to the point, sometimes cryptic, but they always ended with the same brief phrase: 'The world is in truth a carnival of joy.'

On one such occasion, a note was given to Govinda, asking him to make a pilgrimage after Jayananda's death to the Ma Tara shrine in the high foothills of the Himalayas. Govinda questioned the master as to why, and Jayananda responded in writing that the reason would become as manifest as the noon-day sun.

The afternoon of the day that he passed away, Jayananda wrote what was to be his last note. It was addressed to Govinda, and it read, simply: "O Divine One, take our message of liberating joy to the world." Govinda had wanted to ask the master to be more explicit, but he decided to wait until the next day when Jayananda would have more vitality. That day never came.

The news of Jayananda's death caused the entire temple complex to go into a period of extended mourning. For a number of days before the cremation of his body, throngs of devotees from throughout the region poured into the temple's various sanctuaries. Large pictures of the guru were displayed at both the steps of the Ma Tara temple and in the garden areas adjoining his small house. Puja was offered at these sites hourly, and special prayers constantly filled the air. Manindra estimated the number of mourners surrounding his pyre to be in the thousands, and even following the dispersal of his ashes in the Ganges, hundreds of worshipers came daily to see and touch the ground where his body had been consumed.

During this period Manindra did not remain inactive. Several days after the last of Jayananda's funerary rites had been completed, he had discreetly approached Govinda about the transference of community leadership, suggesting that it should be done as quickly as possible so as to give the public the assurance that the movement was stable. Govinda's immediate reaction was one of shocked offense, but he swallowed his tongue and simply told Manindra that he needed some time alone to meditate upon his course of action. He even mentioned that he might possibly go away for a while, perhaps make a pilgrimage to the Himalayan shrines. In spite of Manindra's mild protestation, Govinda recognized that the temple owner was in no position to argue with him, and thus exactly one month after Jayananda's soul had departed the world, Govinda set out from Benares on his journey to the great mountains.

Two months and twenty-three days later, Govinda was high up in the Himalayan foothills. The first part of the trek had been relatively easy. Trains, carts, and horses had taken him as far as the closest shrines, but now that he was well beyond these initial monuments, he had to rely entirely on the strength of his own legs and back. The narrow, windy, and often slippery path upon which he was currently traveling began to climb ever steeper. Govinda noticed the increased strain on his muscles. He also realized that he had to take much deeper breaths in order to maintain a constant pace.

He trudged on for several more miles, periodically stopping to renew his waning strength and take in the breathtaking beauty of the surrounding landscape. With each passing hour the mountain air became increasingly cooler, and it was Govinda's growing hope that it would not be too much longer before he would arrive at the Ma Tara shrine. He was unaware of the structure's exact location, but the description of the terrain around the shrine given to him by several pilgrims whom he had met lower down the mountain, seemed to very much match the scenery he was now encountering.

Since the day he left Benares, two issues had been foremost in Govinda's mind. The first was associated with the question of how to respond to Manindra's offer that he become the movement's new tirthankara. For one thing, when it came to the question of religion, Govinda knew just how different Manindra and Jayananda's attitudes and approaches were, and while he could certainly sympathize with the owner's desire to make of the movement something that could revive a spiritually declining Hinduism and give it a new sense of political and social purpose, he also feared that in so doing he might not be able to remain completely true to Jayananda's vision.

On the other hand, it was undoubtedly true that Govinda did not know exactly what specific teachings and doctrines could be said to have constituted Jayananda's path. To the deceased avatar, everything seemed to have had a metaphorical interpretation. Moreover, he had held a variety of different and seemingly contradictory views on just about all positions. Was he an advocate of advaita monism? Was he a dualist? Was he a devout bhakta? Was he a sanyasin? Was he a gopi playing in a world of spiritually erotic lila? Govinda knew that the answers to all of these questions were both yes and no.

If Shri Jayananda had been more clear, and directly appointed someone as his heir, he would not be in this position. If the tirthankara had wanted an official successor and an official doctrine would he not have made his choices unequivocal by putting them in writing rather than relying on symbolic gestures? Maybe his only purpose was to perform lila here on earth. Perhaps there was no designated objective involving the renewal or revitalization of anyone or anything.

His second problem concerned the doctrine of the secret door. Was it only to be understood from the perspective of divine lila? Although Govinda never for one moment doubted Jayananda's spiritual powers, he still became anxious when he thought about such matters. Why could he only open up to his master when he was entranced? Why did he sometimes intuit within himself a lingering ambivalence towards him? And what sense did it make for one to be frustrated with an avatar?

Govinda stopped his march. This time he sat down at the edge of the trail and softly closed his eyes. *Hopefully I will receive some answers at Ma Tara's shrine*, he thought.

The short rest gave his tired legs some much needed relief, and he was briefly tempted to tarry longer. His head, however, told him that he had to move on. Shortly thereafter, he was once again on his feet heading up the trail.

Govinda traversed a sharp bend that skirted a dangerous precipice and scanned the trail as it stretched out in front of him In the distance he could discern, with some difficulty, the contours of a human figure moving in his direction.

The figure came closer. Govinda recognized that the object of his inspection was a naked sadhu. From head to feet the holy man's entire body was smeared with thick swathes of grey ash. His long beard was moist and matted. In his right hand he held the shaft of a wooden trident. Attached to the staff's middle prong by a thin cotton cord was a miniature wooden drum that rhythmically bounced both up and down and from side to side as the sadhu ambled irrevocably forward.

"Ram Ram," exclaimed the elderly sadhu as soon as the two men were within speaking distance.

Govinda dipped his head slightly forward and brought his hands together at his mouth. "Ram, Ram," he repeated.

"What is your destination?" the sadhu inquired.

"I am looking for the shrine of Ma Tara. I have been told by several travelers that it is situated somewhere nearby. Do you know its location?"

The sadhu placed the end of his crooked staff firmly on the hard ground and examined Govinda with his probing eyes. Govinda for his part instinctively understood the nature of the inspection and preempted the sadhu's question. "I am a pujari from the Ma Tara temple in Benares," he said.

"That is Shri Jayananda's temple, is it not?" asked the sadhu.

"Yes," Govinda affirmed. "Shri Jayananda has recently attained his absolute deliverance, and I am making a pilgrimage to Ma Tara's shrine in his honor."

The sadhu raised his free hand to his balding head and rubbed vigorously. "I knew Shri Jayananda when he was just a small boy," he stated. "He was a simple village lad named Gopala when I taught him the secrets of the Shiva lingam. Who would have guessed that he would depart this world of pain and suffering before I would? But, as we know, everything is in Lord Shiva's hands. There is nothing that he does not control. It is said that when some man or animal is born, it is as if the creature has a noose tied around its neck and has then been thrown off that mountain top." He pointed to a massive peak on the other side of the valley. "We just don't know how long the rope is."

Govinda wondered what the sadhu had meant by the 'secrets of the Shiva lingam.' However, he did not bother to question the older man. He was extremely tired, and he definitely wanted to arrive at the shrine before sunset. A lengthy discussion with an aging sadhu was not on his agenda for this day. He merely nodded in agreement and re-asked his question.

"You will find the entrance to Ma Tara's shrine some two

to three miles up this trail," the holy man replied. "At a spot
where two large trees converge, there is a patch of thick undergrowth. Just on the other side of that undergrowth there is
another path. It is extremely narrow and easy to miss, especially in dim light. It leads back into a small ravine where the
shrine is located."

"You have been most helpful, sadhuji."

The sadhu was not finished. "Since it will soon be getting
dark, I would suggest that you wait until morning. We can
spend the night together in this small clearing." He gestured
to a nearby stretch of dirt and grass. "It has been quite some
time since I have had the pleasure of human company."

"I greatly appreciate your concern," Govinda said, "but I
do want to reach the shrine today rather than tomorrow. And
with your detailed instructions, I am certain that I will not lose
my way."

"As you wish," said the sadhu.

Govinda again exchanged salutations with the holy man
and started the last leg of his climb up the mountainside.

Just as the sun was dipping behind the western ridges,
Govinda reached the location described to him by the sadhu.
He identified the two trees and, after a closer inspection, spotted a small indentation in the undergrowth. *The new path*, he
thought.

His arrival at the spot confirmed his assumption. He
pushed through some of the foliage with his hands and found
himself on a much narrower stretch of dirt which he could see
was partially covered by a number of fallen trees and patches
of sprawling vegetation.

A short distance forward the track made a steep descent.
The footing became treacherous. Govinda walked slowly for
quite some time without seeing any sign of a shrine. His
breathing became more rapid, and he started to experience occasional palpitations which increased in intensity with each
passing minute. Only when he could finally see the dim outline
of a building did he begin to relax.

He drew ever closer to the silhouetted monument.
Govinda noticed a flickering light coming from the building's

entrance. *Someone must be inside.* Again his heart began to beat irregularly.

He was nearing the first of the nine steps that led up to the shrine's opening. He took several more paces and put his foot down on the initial stone slab. There was a sudden movement in the doorway. He looked up to see a red-robed woman coming down the steps towards him. He immediately recognized who it was—Rukhmini.

He had never formally met Rukhmini, but he was very much aware of her friendship with Jayananda. The avatar had occasionally spoken to him of his affection for the bhairavi, but Govinda had always been somewhat suspicious of the woman. Perhaps this was due to some of the rumors he had heard when he first joined the community, or perhaps it was the fear that Jayananda shared special secrets with Rukhmini. Whatever the case, the moment he saw her, negative thoughts entered his mind.

Rukhmini spoke first. "I have been expecting you, Govinda." She looked boldly at the disciple.

Govinda was caught off guard. He stood stationary on the first step and sputtered out his words. "How can that be?"

"Shri Jayananda informed me that he would send you to me," Rukhmini responded.

The bhairavi descended to the third step and stopped. She reached down into her red robe, took out a small piece of wrinkled paper, and extended it towards Govinda. "Here, read this," she said.

Govinda took the paper and cautiously unwrapped it. He began to read. Instantly he recognized his master's uneven script. The note was addressed to him: "Ma is my mother; I am your mother; and you will become the mother of many. As the sun follows the moon in the sky, so must the son always follow his mother and in so doing devour her."

Govinda read the words several times.

Rukhmini understood that Govinda was having difficulty grasping the cryptic message. "It is presently upon you to fulfill your duty as the next tirthankara," she bluntly stated. "Like Shri Jayananda, you must become a student of all the spiritual paths. When you have mastered them all, then you must teach these paths to the children of India. But most importantly, you must find those truly enlightened souls and teach them the secrets of the divine lila, the love play of the great Mother. That is why you have been incarnated, O agnivesha. Shri Jayananda was the divine spark. Now you must become the forest fire."

Govinda wrinkled his brow and drew his head back. Only Jayananda had ever referred to him as an agnivesha.

"I am here to initiate you into the secrets of the tantric path. This is the path that the enlightened souls of humanity so desperately need to know. This is the knowledge of the divine feminine, the Motherhood of God, reserved for the end of the yuga when the great souls can release themselves from the bondage of fear and shame. This is the secret door which Shri Jayananda has unlocked for you. Now you are the divine key that will open it for others."

Rukhmini returned to the top of the steps. At the doorway she turned and beckoned Govinda with her left hand. "Come," she said.

Govinda could feel that same mesmerizing pull that he had so often experienced when he was with Jayananda. He obeyed the bhairavi and followed her into the shrine.

Chapter 28

The meeting hall was filled to capacity. Every one of the nearly five hundred seats was occupied, and the thin corridor of floor space that stretched around the sides and back of the building was likewise packed with energetic followers. All of the men, whether seated or standing, were rife with expectation. On this night they would formally be introduced to the movement's new tirthankara. They were currently being addressed by Manindra, but their sense of enthusiastic anticipation could not be completely contained as was indicated by the low but constant buzzing sound that emanated from all corners of the room. From his position on the far right side of the slightly elevated stage, the youthful Govinda looked out at the sea of white-clothed enthusiasts and remembered that it was not so terribly long ago he himself was part of such an audience.

Manindra was concluding the last portion of his welcoming speech. Govinda braced himself for the words that would bring him to his feet and mark the beginning of a new phase in his life. He rapidly went over in his mind the main ideas that he wanted to cover in his inaugural address.

As soon as he heard his new title 'Swami Satyananda,' Govinda and his two attendants were moving towards Manindra. When they were several feet away from the temple owner, the crowd began to let out cheers of "long live Satyananda." The chanting continued. Manindra placed a garland of white and yellow chrysanthemums around the new tirthankara's neck.

Satyananda bowed graciously to his benefactor and then seated himself on the large cushion dominating the center of the stage. Manindra and the attendants gracefully removed themselves from the limelight. The new leader closed his eyes and quietly waited for the shouting to subside.

In contrast to the manner in which Jayananda had dressed for such occasions, Satyananda was attired in a full-length brown robe, drawn together at his waist by an even darker cotton sash. Atop his head sat a neatly folded cream-colored turban.

When the noise was barely noticeable, Satyananda opened his eyes and spoke. "Om Tat Sat." These three words of invocation established complete silence.

"The first thing I must tell you as your new tirthankara is that while he is no longer with us in material form, the spirit of our beloved Shri Jayananda has by no means departed. And just as his great spirit remains eternally present amongst us, so does the spirit of our great mother India."

The room filled with applause, but Satyananda quickly raised his right hand into the air and quieted the audience. "As long as her people do not abandon their spirituality, the Indian nation cannot be destroyed. She may be conquered physically, she may toil for long periods of time in material poverty, but she will always maintain her spiritual strength. And in the end, if she heroically perseveres, the Indian nation will be victorious. For the spirit is everlasting, and the message of God is eternal. These primal truths have always been part of her faithful heritage. Throughout the ages, the great sages and holy men have continued to appear from her bosom to remind the people of this truth. Let them not forget that they are the children of the sages . . .

"Such a one was our beloved Shri Jayananda. Born into a simple but devout village family, he grew up enchanted with the stories of our nation's wondrous saints and heroes. But his path to enlightenment was not to be an easy one. For many years he struggled mightily to understand the truth. Eventually, he began to experience visions and to behold marvelous things. Slowly, the secret of his own inner nature began to become apparent to him . . .

"Finally, Ma Tara herself became his teacher. The divine Mother of us all gracefully revealed her mystical secrets to him, and he became completely enthralled in the rapture of her presence. Gladly, he would have remained the rest of his life alone with her. But he also came to realize that he had a sacred duty to spread the glad tidings of his divine Mother so that the material manifestation of her worldly family, this great nation we call India, would continue its spiritualizing mission among the civilizations of the world. Thus did our beloved Shri Jayananda take on the roll of the tirthankara."

Satyananda paused to allow the audience to once more express its emotions. After several waves of applause, and an equal number of intermittent chants, he proceeded with his oration.

"Many people came to see Shri Jayananda. And it was not so much to hear his words, although these were filled with the divine spirit, but rather to be in his presence. For it is not only what is spoken, but the transcending personality of the speaker, which is beyond words, that truthfully attracts the soul of another . . .

"While still a student I, myself, came to hear of this tirthankara and by chance went to see him. And although at first I did not understand his words, I was instantly drawn to him by the power of his person. It was as if my soul could sense what my mind could not fathom. Eventually I sought him out and sat in his presence, and it was then that I realized that the truth could become manifest in a human being. One glance, one touch, was enough to convey this eternal mystery. I became his follower."

Satyananda reached out and took hold of a brass cup that sat on the floor next to him and quickly wet his mouth.

"And what did I learn from this man?" he asked after he had returned the container to the floor. "What were the divine truths of which he was the human embodiment?

"The first and most significant of Shri Jayananda's teachings is that true religion is synonymous with renunciation. Enjoyment of the world and enjoyment of God are incompatible. Man cannot have both. Now does this mean that all good Hindus must become celibate and live lives of abject poverty and abstinence? Of course not. Only a few are called to such a life. By this very reason of divine grace, and as examples to the rest of mankind, there are men who can live without caring one iota for all the riches and fame that the universe has to offer.

So, a religious man can live in the world. But, . . . and here Shri Jayananda was uncompromising, a religious man lives in the world from a sense of duty rather than from a desire for pleasure. He raises a family and tends to his business affairs out of the love of God and not out of concern for himself. And in such renunciation, a man maintains his true virility. He becomes the master over himself. He is not pulled down by the temptations of the ever fickle world of maya . . .

This was the reason Shri Jayananda took a wife—to serve as an example of true renunciation—and in so doing to transform a simple village girl from an object of desire into a subject of the most pure devotion. He allowed Chandramani to become the Ma Devi that we all know and adore."

Satyananda could sense within himself a growing awareness of strength and control, and this confidence became gradually apparent to his listeners. They had increasingly become hypnotized by his powerful voice and charismatic energy. Their own prior boisterousness left them to be replaced by intense stares of admiration.

"Now, as many of you know, on occasion Shri Jayananda took the guise of a woman. He dressed like a woman; he spoke like a woman; he behaved like a woman. As a result of these actions it has been suggested in some quarters that he was less than spiritually pure, if not worse."

Satyananda temporarily halted his discourse. Then in a voice that was even more authoritative in tone, he proceeded.

"Let me make it very clear what Shri Jayananda was doing. That great tirthankara was manifesting in his person the fact that we should look upon all women as manifestations of the great Mother, that we should rid our hearts of any notion of carnal lust . . . Think of the high nature of a life from which all carnality has been removed, a life that can look upon every woman as an incarnation of Ma, the protector of the human race. This was his meaning, for he knew that only those souls who hold in their hearts such ideals of purity will be able to traverse the path of self realization."

Satyananda took another sip of water.

"And this leads me to Shri Jayananda's next teaching: One should not be concerned with doctrines or dogmas. True religion is self-realization, the growing awareness that the divine is within oneself. Indeed, each individual self is but a drop of that glorious ocean of being that we sometimes call Brahman and at other times Ma Tara . . .

"Whatever we call this ultimate reality, knowledge of it and it alone is the highest knowledge. Secondary knowledge is gained through the senses and worship, but essential knowledge comes only through self-realization of that Absolute . . .

"The Absolute Brahman is self-sufficient; it is without cause. In truth, Brahman is all there is. And, as Shri Jayananda knew and taught, each individual soul, that which we call the true self, is identical with that Brahman. As finite beings, we can never express the Absolute. But we are that Absolute; we are that Brahman. We know this from experience and not from words or formulas. So each of us must continually strive to realize in ourselves what Shri Jayananda realized: that the knower and the known are one. The gods that we see in meditation are seen through the power of our own selves . . .

"And also, my brothers," Satyananda now exhorted the faithful, "Shri Jayananda taught us that we should not be satisfied with isolated self-realization. We should also be concerned in caring for and serving the poor and dispossessed among us. And when we think about this, we should see such service as a natural extension of self-realization, for in becoming aware that our own self is one with Brahman, it naturally follows that all souls are one with Brahman. There is, in fact, no other. All men are our brothers, and all women are our mothers. This is why Shri Jayananda could stand bathed in tears before those women which society would not touch and cry: 'Mother, in one form you are in the street, and in another form you are the universe. Mother, I salute you.'"

There were a few in the audience who did not feel completely comfortable with this particular interpretation of Jayananda's teachings, but rather than demonstrate any visible sign of dissent, they courteously remained quiet and waited for Satyananda to move on. The new tirthankara could intuit this ambivalence. Hence he hastily returned to the thread with which he had initiated his speech — one he knew would be acceptable to his listener's ears.

"Some of you have asked me what destiny awaits our beloved Hindu religion," he continued. "Similarly, many have wondered how a religion that has for centuries lived under foreign political control can have any future except that of servitude. To this I answer that the time is not far away when India's spiritual heritage will break free from its political bondage and reap great harvests throughout the world."

Satyananda halted to again allow the audience to release its energy. Waves of applause rippled through the building accompanied by a chorus of shouts: "Victory to Mother India; Long live Hindu dharma."

"But how can that be?" many of you might ask. "How can a religion that has been so denigrated, so emasculated by foreign oppressors arise from the ashes?"

Satyananda's voice was beginning to strain. "The answer is not difficult to find. It is written in the pages of history. Ironically, it is written in the pages of the history of that ancient religion which our current masters claim to represent: Christianity."

There was not a man in the audience who did not inwardly react in some way to the word "Christianity." To a large number it brought feelings of anger, to a few pangs of conscience. But whatever their inner response, they all now listened with heightened intensity.

"If we look back to the time when Jesus of Nazareth was walking this Earth, what political conditions do we find?" Satyananda asked. "We find a nation of people hemmed in by the greatest political might in the world: the Roman Empire.

And these people, the Jewish nation, were forced to concentrate and focus all of their energy on maintaining their spiritual traditions in the face that overwhelming external political power. Yet, it was from this very condition of servitude that Christianity arose and eventually conquered its oppressors. On the shoulders of Jesus a great tidal wave of energy radiated outward. In him was embodied all that was the best and greatest in his own people. He himself became a spiritual impetus for the future, not only for his own race but for the entire world."

A new buzz of excitement started to spread throughout the assemblage as its members grasped where their new tirthankara's words were taking them.

"And so it will be with our Hindu tradition, for like the Jews who were oppressed for centuries, our great nation has brought forth from its bosom a spirit that embodies the same type of divine energy as was manifest in the person of Jesus. In Shri Jayananda, we once again find the incarnation of the eternal spirit. With him, a new wave of divine energy has been released into the world, and it is now our duty and our privilege to cause this energy to radiate outward from our great Mother India to all parts of that world. As your tirthankara I pledge myself to that goal, and I also ask that every man here tonight commit himself to spreading that light, and in so doing, to return a strong and vigorous India to its rightful place among the family of nations."

The eruption that followed Satyananda's last words confirmed the powerful emotional chord he had struck with his followers. Rather than quell that emotion, the new leader allowed for its full expression by raising his clinched right hand above his head and thrusting it towards the ceiling.

Chapter 29

Satyananda said farewell to his visi-
tors and calmly observed their horse drawn carriage pull away
from the temple entrance. He watched until the conveyance
was almost out of sight. He waved and then turned and headed
back into the compound. He had planned to return directly to
the office and continue working on his upcoming speech, but
when he was nearly halfway to the house, he spontaneously
decided that he would spend a few quiet moments alone. He
set out in the direction of the pine grove.

Not quite five years had passed since Jayananda's death
and Satyananda's assumption of leadership. During that time
the movement had shown tremendous growth. Numerous distinguished disciples and admirers had been incorporated into
its ranks, and several temple complexes from regions as far
away as Orissa and Madras had lent their support.

While some of the gain was due to Manindra's financial
shrewdness, there was little doubt in most of the members'
minds that it was primarily the oratorical skills and driving will
of Satyananda that was responsible for the success. True, there
were some who felt that the new tirthankara had used his position essentially to promote himself rather than Jayananda, but
these voices were in a minority. To the rank and file
Satyananda was not only a master of the Vedanta but a great

spiritual warrior, a leader who was once again reaffirming Hinduism's legitimate place amongst the world's religions. Soon he would soon be venturing across the ocean to lecture Europeans on the nobility of his ancient heritage.

Satyananda reached the grassy knoll that signaled the beginning of the pine grove. Images of Jayananda trickled into his mind. It was here that the two men had so often sat together and talked of the eternal verities, had saturated themselves in the excitement of the divine lila, had basked in the joy of each other's presence. And it was also here that the avatar had passed on to his protégé the deepest secrets of their true natures and identities.

So immersed in these thoughts was Satyananda that at first he did not even notice the figure sitting under the first of the pine trees. It was only when he was virtually on top of her that he was jolted from his daydreaming and recognized the visitor.

The bhairavi had aged dramatically since Satyananda had last seen her. The life of a wandering sanyasin had taken its toll on both her skin and hair. The former was parched and scaly, while the latter had not only turned a dirty grey, it was also so matted and tangled as to look like one solid mass of sludge. Nevertheless, the dynamic spirit that had always dominated the woman's eyes was still present, and when Satyananda looked at her, Rukhmini's bluish-grey irises instantly lit up.

"Namaskar Govinda," she said.

Satyananda did not return the greeting. He was unprepared for this encounter and could not find the appropriate words.

Rukhmini, in contrast, was eager to make conversation. "I see that you have gained many followers," she remarked.

"The movement is growing," Satyananda affirmed in a low voice. "I believe Shri Jayananda would be pleased."

Rukhmini let out a scowling laugh. "How would he be pleased when you have betrayed him so?"

Satyananda's jaw tightened. His shoulders and head tilted forward. Anger flared from his eyes.

Rukhmini did not wait for him to speak. "Shri Jayananda's mission was the liberation of enlightened souls from fear and

shame by means of the divine lila. You have made him into a
false idol. Like Manindra, you are more concerned with your
own image in the eyes of the world and its rulers than you are
with the truths that became flesh in Shri Jayananda. You call it
'the movement,' and represent it as India, but in truth it is your
own resentful selves that you propagate."

"That is not so," Satyananda loudly declared. He could
feel the heat rushing into his cheeks.

"Isn't it? I have heard your speeches, and I can see what
you have done. You have abandoned the personality of god for
an abstract ideology; you have abandoned the spiritual eroti-
cism of the divine lila for the platitudes of the Vedanta; you
have abandoned the life of mystical solitude for the life of social activism; you have abandoned Ma Tara for your own cas-
trated Shiva. And the irony is that you don't see that in
abandoning Shri Jayananda's path you have adopted the path
of your conquerors. You are only trying to beat them at their
own game."

Satyananda quietly took in the bhairavi's words. His hos-
tility gradually mounted, and by the time she had finished he
was filled with righteous indignation.

"What do you know of Shri Jayananda?" he sneered. "All
you ever did was try to beguile and corrupt him with your insidious and superstitious ideas, just as you tried to enchant me.
The secret path which you so boldly pronounce is nothing but
disguised filth performed in the name of religion."

"Have you forgotten what Shri Jayananda said about the
'knowers' who follow the path of the Vedanta?" Signs of an
ironic smile began forming around the edges of Rukhmini's
mouth. "Do you so easily forget that your tirthankara saw their
doctrines of cosmic illusion and 'not this, not that' as inadequate half truths? Do you not remember that his greatest energies were given to the enlightened ones of his inner circle
through the performance of lila?"

"You have twisted his words and his meaning," Satyananda
answered. "As he often said: 'When the lotus opens, the bees
come of their own accord to seek the honey. So let the lotus of
your own character become open and it fruits will then be

come manifest.' . . . The fruits of your character have become manifest, Rukhmini, and they are like rotten bananas."
The woman threw her head back and her eyes widened. "It is you, Govinda, who have twisted the tirthankara's words," she retorted. "Next, you will be telling me that Shri Jayananda did not embody the spirit of the eternal Mother, that he was not an incarnation of Ma Tara but merely some Rama-like warrior whose aim was to cast out of India the Ravanas of our time." The bhairavi's voice was beginning to show signs of fatigue.
Satyananda pressed his attack. "It is obvious that you never grasped Shri Jayananda's deeper understanding of the divine Mother. How could you? You who have discarded the role of mother for one of female eunuch. If you want to understand it, just go into Ma Tara's temple. Go to the spot where Shri Jayananda spent countless hours alone with the goddess. If you can find the humility to surrender your own preconceptions, you will notice that Ma carries a sword and she is mounted atop her lord Shiva. It was from those very visible signs that Shri Jayananda came to his understanding of the nature of divine motherhood. From Ma herself he learned to realize that the divine Mother is both nurturer and warrior, mother and father."
Rukhmini shook her head in dismay. "Do you deny that Shri Jayananda taught the doctrine of the secret door?" Do you deny he revealed to you that you are an agnivesha, and that like your divine father you were to be the keeper of that sacred entrance and a transmitter of its seed?"
Satyananda was ready. "Indeed Shri Jayananda revealed to me that I am an agnivesha and that I am a keeper of that secret door," he shouted, "but the secret door to which you refer is a creation of your own childish mind. The secret door of which Shri Jayananda made me the keeper is the secret knowledge of his true self. And in this new age that door is to be opened to all who would accept it."
"You must remember to whom you are speaking." Rukhmini had regained her composure. "I am not some ignorant starry-eyed follower who wants to hear that his mother

India is destined for greatness. I knew Shri Jayananda. I initiated him into the secrets of the tantric path."

"But you never completed the initiation, did you." Satyananda widened his face. His head bobbed ever-so-slightly.

"And the fact that the last step was never concluded shows that Shri Jayananda was aware of what you really are. You are woman, not mother; you are bewitcher."

"Then why was it that Shri Jayananda spent so much time with me, became my pupil and finally a master of my teachings? Are you saying that your avatar was capable of being fooled and beguiled?"

Satyananda lost no time in supplying his answer. "For the same reason that he mingled with prostitutes," he said. "Even in one like you he could see the potential of divine motherhood. He mastered your teachings so that he could understand their power, for without an understanding of their power he knew they could not be vanquished."

Rukhmini again shook her head and then got to her feet. The two adversaries were now standing face to face.

"Dismiss me if you like," Satyananda snapped, "but you have no power over me now. I must admit that at one time I was confused about some of Shri Jayananda's teachings, but after that night at Ma Tara's shrine when you so treacherously attempted to snare me in your tantric web, I knew something was terribly wrong. So upon my return to the temple, I sat before Ma's image for an entire day and meditated upon the master's final words: 'Ma is my mother; I am your mother; and you will become the mother of many. As the sun follows the moon in the sky, so must the son always follow his mother and in so doing devour her.'

I waited patiently for an answer, and finally Ma revealed to me the secret meaning of those words. Shri Jayananda appeared as my mother to liberate me from the fear of both man and woman, father and mother. For as the father would castrate me, so would the mother devour me. Only self-realization allows the son to become both his own father and his own mother. And thus I came to see not only who I am, but who you really are. You are none other than Ravana, returned in female form, who would take our beloved Sita of self-realization from us in the form of your insidious doctrines. This I will never allow."

The bhairavi's eyes remained intense. "You have become ensnared in your own vain imaginings."

"You seem to have forgotten that Shri Jayananda chose me to be the new tirthankara," Satyananda said with an air of self-satisfaction.

Rukhmini turned to leave and then halted. "It is true," she scowled as she again faced Satyananda, "that Shri Jayananda never completed the last step of the tantric initiation with me . . . but you know who completed it."

For the first time since he had left home and entered the temple complex, Satyananda had the desire to strike another human being. He raised his right hand and clenched his fist. "Leave," he yelled. "Leave right now and never return to this temple."

"Yes, I will leave," the bhairavi said, "but the truth is the truth, and though it may take some time to become manifest, in the end Shri Jayananda's real teachings will again be revealed."

Rukhmini lifted her cloak and walked away. As she approached the banks of the Ganges, she reached down into her soiled bag and pulled out the image of the entwined Radha and Krishna. She gazed at it briefly and then hurled it into the river. "All things return," she whispered.

When Rukhmini was finally out of sight Satyananda began his short journey back to the mansion. He pondered the opening lines for the speech he would soon begin writing. He was consumed by the feeling of absolute certitude.